A Murder
at the Potter Hotel

by
Annie J. Dahlgren
and Neal P. Graffy

Annie Dahlgren

D1417634

Copyright

December 2015, edition 2015
El Barbareño Publishing
Santa Barbara, CA

Cover Design by Annie Gallup

Layout by Anna Lafferty,

All photos courtesy Neal Graffy Collection, except top of page 54, 55 courtesy Peter Jordano.

ISBN: 978-0-9821636-5-8

NOTE:
This is a work of fiction. Names, characters and incidents are either the product of the author's imagination or are used fictitiously.

Thank You

Thank you **Monte Schulz**, for the great gift of your time and knowledge.

Thank you **Johnny Ruffin,** for sharing the depth and delight of a ten year old boy.

Thank you **David and Patty West**, for reading every draft and offering encouragement and enthusiasm when needed most.

Thank you **Annie Gallup** and **Anna Lafferty** for your creativity and professionalism.

Thank you **family and friends** for the wonderfulness that is family and friends.

Thank you **Leontine Birabent Phelan** for living an interesting life and befriending young Neal.

Forwerd

❧

*Neal & Leontine,
Easter 1976*

I was fourteen, with a lucrative business of gardening and house cleaning, when I climbed the four steps at 820 Santa Barbara Street to meet my newest client, Leontine Birabent Phelan. She seemed ancient at seventy-five but even older was her home, the Rochin Adobe, built in 1854 by her grandfather, José Marie Rochin, from the ruins of the crumbling Santa Barbara *presidio*. As we made our way through her house to the kitchen I could see every room was filled with strange, unusual and curious objects. I would soon learn these were rare and wonderful relics of California and Santa Barbara history.

But the greatest treasure in the house was my new friend. Each Saturday would be spent working at her house, and the highlight of the day was the lunch break where she would entertain me with tales of old Santa Barbara – and she had much to tell. This began my love affair with Santa Barbara history. Her family lineage extended back to José Francisco Ortega, the first *comandante* of the Spanish *presidio* and she had no shortage of stories of her forbearers as well as her own life. She'd ridden in stagecoaches, carriages, and on horseback and then witnessed the end of that era when the first automobile in Santa Barbara chugged down State

Street. She had seen the first aeroplanes in death-defying exhibitions in Hope Ranch, witnessed the birth of Lockheed Aviation on West Beach and years later flew in a jet herself, to Hawaii. Later still she watched a man land on the moon.

Leontine, or Lulubelle as I came to call her, was in fact a piano teacher, until 1912 when she became a film editor for the American Film Company only a few months after their arrival in Santa Barbara. Living on the 500 block of State Street, she was in the thick of the destruction as the June 29, 1925 earthquake rocked the town, recalling every sensation as she described the day for me. One of our favorite topics was the great Potter Hotel, and her vivid memories of how it was built, how she experienced it, and how it died. Quite fitting that this is where these stories begin.

Leontine and I would remain the best of friends for the next twenty-six years until her death at 101 and half years of age. Nearly five decades have passed since our first meeting and I continue to carry her stories and experiences in my heart.

Friends observing the gestation of this book have wondered, exactly which parts are history and which are mystery. Many who have attended my lectures have heard me joke that "I never let facts get in the way of a good story". Yet, as a historian, I feel a responsibility to verify the truth of what I've read or been told and spend countless hours chasing minutia toward that end.

What fun to now work on this book with Annie J. Dahlgren and relate many facts about daily life in 1908 Santa Barbara and the visit of the Great White Fleet, and at the same time imagine other incidents as they could have unfolded had they actually occurred. I can only honestly say that much of what is presented really happened, and the rest is a good story.

So dear reader, enjoy the tale of what did happen along with what could have happened as Leontine and her friends embark on their first Santa Barbara History Mystery.

Neal Graffy
Santa Barbara
November, 2015

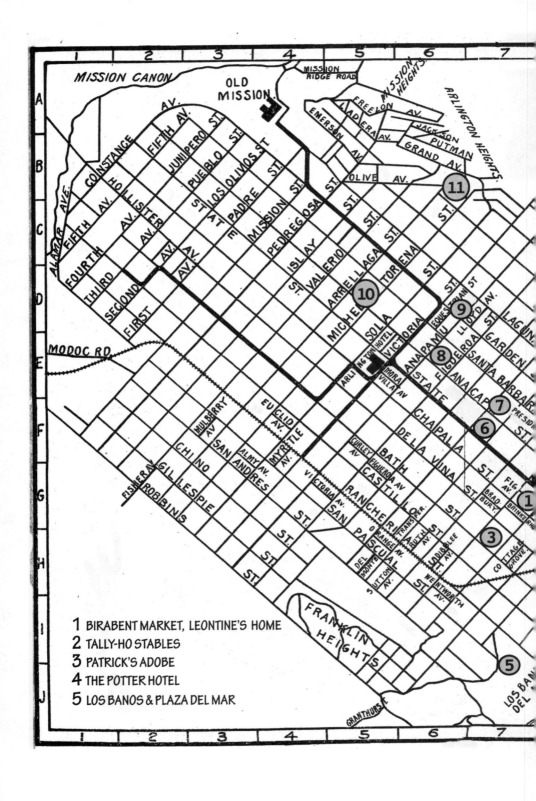

1 BIRABENT MARKET, LEONTINE'S HOME
2 TALLY-HO STABLES
3 PATRICK'S ADOBE
4 THE POTTER HOTEL
5 LOS BANOS & PLAZA DEL MAR

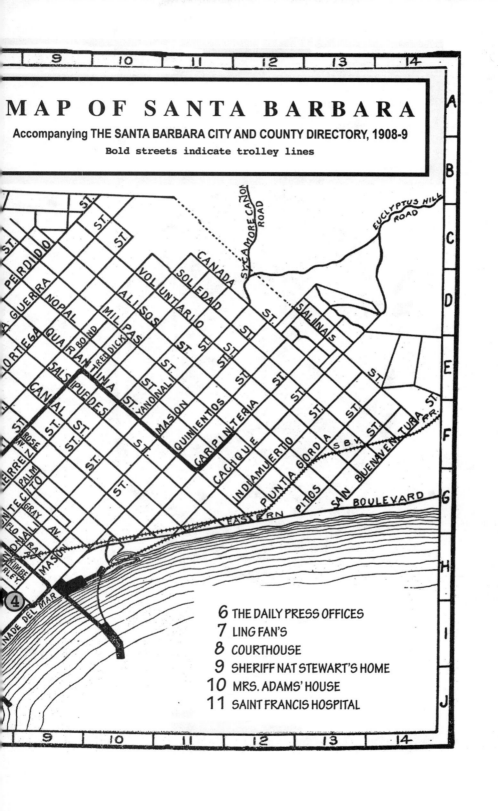

MAP OF SANTA BARBARA

Accompanying **THE SANTA BARBARA CITY AND COUNTY DIRECTORY, 1908-9**

Bold streets indicate trolley lines

6 THE DAILY PRESS OFFICES
7 LING FAN'S
8 COURTHOUSE
9 SHERIFF NAT STEWART'S HOME
10 MRS. ADAMS' HOUSE
11 SAINT FRANCIS HOSPITAL

Chapter I

If Leontine's parents had chosen her name to instill in her something fierce they had not missed the mark by far. Not fierceness exactly, which brings with it an element of malice, but strength, certainly, and deep powers of focused concentration. It was surprising to her therefore, to regain consciousness and realize she had fainted, a behavior she thought reserved for more delicate girls. Even in that moment she blamed the corset – a tortuous garment detested by all. She decided then and there to abandon it forever. On several recent occasions she had ventured out without it and found that it was apparently not noticeable. That, or people successfully disguised any negative reaction. Either way she saw no point in causing herself harm if no one was going to give her credit for it. In addition, she had made the decision to overload a small wagon rather than half-load a big one and then learned that her preferred mare at the Talley Ho Stables, a patient and docile draft horse named Lindy Sue, was otherwise occupied.

The Talley Ho Livery stable was situated on the sunny east side of State Street between Haley and Cota Streets in downtown Santa Barbara. On this side of State Street the storefronts of the mainly Victorian buildings included canvas or wooden awnings extending over concrete sidewalks rather than windows and doorways that crowded the pedestrian walkway as did the businesses on the shady west side of the street.

Leontine loved the smell of the leather saddles and bridles, the hay and the well-cared-for animals themselves. Though the name of the establishment had a decidedly British flavor, the livery stable was in fact owned by one Diego Ramirez. In the same way the business name obscured the truth of the lineage of its owner, Diego's Mexican name did not accurately represent his Chumash Indian ancestry. The secularization of the California mission system some eighty years earlier had locally resulted in tossing what had remained of the indigenous population from their regimented existences in the Indian Village adjacent to the Old Mission and scattered them among neighboring ranchos and small towns. There they worked mainly has cooks, nannies, vaqueros and laborers. A few, like Diego, attempted to make a success of some enterprise or other in the ever-expanding communities along the central coast of California. Though their ancient names had disappeared almost immediately, their native culture was taking longer to fade. Nevertheless, it was by now very nearly just as much gone.

Diego was short and square and strong, and though the lines in his face suggested he had seen at least forty years, not one gray strand could be found in the long braid gathered at his back. Diego had warned Leontine that the boxes of dry goods and tins might be unwieldy, however well lashed, especially given the fact that the only horse currently available was Otis, a towering quarter horse of uneven temperament. He was a relatively new arrival at the Tally Ho and therefore unfamiliar with the path to the Potter Hotel where her delivery was bound. Diego's apprehensions proved accurate as Leontine was forced to scurry back and forth between the teetering boxes and the nervous animal. It was a hot day, as it sometimes could be in April, and she felt sweaty and anxious and short of breath. Her ultimate destination dictated an elevated level of fashion not consistent with the task at hand and layers of fabric from her long skirt and undergarments twisted around her legs and caught on her buttoned up shoes. Her chosen hat was definitely more stylish than functional and the fitted velvet jacket that dropped past her hips added yet another layer of material to trap heat generated by her frenetic activity. And she was wearing the corset. She managed to maneuver over the wooden bridge at Mission Creek on Cota Street, turned and started down Bath Street toward the oceanfront, and then collapsed.

Upon opening her eyes, Leontine struggled to focus clearly on a boy of ten or eleven years leaning over her and studying her face.

"You're the piano teacher," said the boy.

Leontine rolled onto one elbow and sat up awkwardly, her feet stretched out straight in front of her. Though the dirt lane was packed and solid near the center, she was closer to the edge of the road where loose gravel mixed with sparse weeds and wild grass and the dirt turned to dust that blew about and seeped into everything. She saw her hat just out of reach, its white plumes and ribbon buried in powdery earth. She leaned in that direction to snatch it up but moved her hand to her forehead instead, uncaring that her stylishly upswept tresses had come undone and left her mounds of chestnut hair tumbling past her shoulders.

"Am I okay?"

The boy looked around for someone more informed to answer the question, but there was no one. "Can you stand up?"

Leontine thought about it for a moment from where she was. "Not yet."

"Should I go get someone?" he offered.

"Not yet."

Leontine did not particularly care for children, and for their insistent and deluded mothers even less, but the piano lessons gave purpose to her love of music and provided welcome change from the more mundane, if also more lucrative, tasks of running the Birabent Market. She focused now on this admittedly caring young boy. He was skinny, the light brown hair beneath his wool cap stick-straight and tending toward unruliness. He peered at her from behind wire-rimmed glasses that magnified his blue eyes in a distorting manner and he wore an adult look of concern on his youthful face that seemed out of place with the knee-length flannel trousers, leggings and rough leather shoes of a child. She then noticed a gangly mutt whining and circling, a look of concern on his mongrel face. His fur was mostly black with a white stripe down his nose and another patch in the long matted fur of his chest that would probably prove to be white as well, were he to have a bath. She held out her hand for the dog to sniff in a gesture of acceptance.

"Careful, Tesla," his young master cautioned. "Good boy."

The dog sniffed her hand and then circled gently once more as if assessing her condition on his own.

"Tesla?" Leontine squinted up at the boy.

"If you have to ask," he answered, "it doesn't matter."

Leontine set about pulling herself to her feet. The child went immediately to her side offering his slight body as support. Grateful for the assistance, she stood and looked around for the horse and wagon. They were fifty yards away, Otis munching grass at the side of the road. Leontine checked her surroundings as her fingers set about the task of sweeping her hair back into place, searching for and finding hairpins in the tangle, seemingly of their own accord. She was halfway between Cota and Haley Streets and didn't have far to go to get to the Potter back entrance, but she wasn't going to do it in this corset.

She asked, "Do you live around here? What's your name?"

"Patrick." He wiped his nose with the back of his hand.

They were situated in front of the crumbling ruins of an old adobe dwelling. As long as Leontine could remember no one had lived in the house. It was set well back from the street and the grounds were wild and overgrown with mustard grass, wild anise and thick, towering dandelion weeds. An earthen walkway curved toward the entrance flanked by the skeletons of long-dead rose bushes. The residence, situated deep in the shadow of a sprawling oak tree, was covered in leaves and dust and bird waste. Sandstone boulders outlined what had undoubtedly once been a well-tended garden, but that was now overrun by one giant nopal cactus plant, its broad fleshy palms budding and endlessly multiplying through the years. Only the vibrant crimson blossoms of a wild bougainvillea plant engulfing the entire north side of the structure provided any color other than varying hues of the earth itself.

"Have you ever been inside?" Leontine asked, tilting her head slightly toward the old adobe.

"No," he said immediately, but something about the way his eyes shifted to the side away from her gaze made her suspect otherwise.

"Would you guard me while I go in there?"

"No. I mean, you can't. You shouldn't. Why do you need to go in there?"

She saw no reason to be coy with the little boy. "I want to take off my corset. I think it made me faint."

Patrick pursed his lips, looked her in the eye for a moment, and then let out a breath. "Okay, but don't touch anything while you're in there."

Leontine was intrigued. She walked up the walkway to the splintering front door while Patrick straightened his back and turned to face the road, serious about protecting her from any harm that might show up. It took her eyes a moment to become accustomed to the dim interior. When they did she gaped at the unexpected scene. A cushioned leather sofa and matching wing chair faced a bricked fireplace and low hearth. Though the leather was faded and cracked it nevertheless appeared soft and inviting. An oval hooked rug defined the area that at one time had probably served as both living room and sleeping quarters. A second room was partially open to the elements as a portion of the roof had burned away in a blaze set long ago. The hole opened up under the spreading branches of the oak tree outside creating the sensation of being in a tree house. The effect was delightful. Along the front wall of this second room beneath two tall deeply-recessed windows stood a long plank table piled with artifacts and instruments and stones and beads and string and pans that gave the room a look something like a cross between a laboratory, a jeweler's workroom and a cabinetmaker's shop all at once.

Leontine peeked out the window to make certain her protector was at his post, then proceeded to unbuttoned the dozen and a half buttons of her black velvet jacket, then the white cotton shirt beneath, and finally the metal clasps of the god-forsaken corset. She dropped the thing on the floor while she buttoned herself up again, then grabbed it up and rolled it into a cylinder that she held behind her skirt as she rejoined Patrick outside. Leontine shaded her eyes and once again registered the location of the horse and wagon.

"I didn't touch anything," she assured him, "but I confess, I wanted to. Thank you for letting me go in there."

Patrick shrugged and looked at his shoes.

She asked, "Do your parents own this house?"

"Nobody does."

Leontine bent and brushed at dust clinging to her skirt. "Well, someone does." She twisted her head around for another look.

"And it's just my dad," the little boy offered. "My mom already died when I was three."

Leontine turned her gaze back to the child, thinking how very sad that someone so young had already experienced an event so devastating.

"How old are you?"

"Ten and a half. How old are you?"

There was something challenging in his question, as if he were striving to keep them on equal footing.

"Twenty-one and a half. Or, three-fourths, I suppose."

The two of them instinctively fell into step heading in the direction of Otis and the wagon. Leontine looked around. She had a little under half a mile to go to get to the Potter Hotel service entrance, and the dirt roads were well packed and relatively free of ruts. On the other hand, the distance between houses was greater the closer one got to the hotel and most of the foot traffic used State or Chapala Streets. If she fainted again no one might notice for a while. She was unaccustomed to feeling so vulnerable and her brow knitted in concern.

"Do you want me to walk with you?" Patrick offered.

Leontine looked down at the boy, relief showing on her face. "I would appreciate it, thank you. Have you been to the Potter Hotel?"

"Not inside."

"Would you like to go inside?"

"Sure I would! Am I allowed?"

Leontine smiled. "Of course. I need to stop in the kitchens and then we'll take the elevator to the top floor."

Patrick's face crinkled into an adorable smile.

Leontine was unaccustomed to being charmed by children, but there was something calm and mature in this boy that stirred her heart, assuming, as she did, that it was borne of the hardship of learning his way in the world without a mother. Patrick pursed his lips and whistled. Tesla appeared seemingly from nowhere and wagged his tail energetically as he trotted along at his master's side. Leontine walked around the wagon, making certain that all of the ropes restraining the merchandise were securely attached to the upright plank lip bolted to the flatbed wagon. Then she gathered the horse's bridle and urged the animal to abandon his snack and get on with the show. Though it was warm, Leontine felt somehow revived, partially from the liberation of being out of the corset, now stashed beneath the wooden seat of the wagon, but even more from the presence of her new friend.

Many people know quite a lot about some particular thing or other. Maybe it's the moon or world history or color or sound. They're drawn to it. Study it. So, too, do they have a sense of "knowing" – almost a "pre-knowledge" as it were – that would sustain and grow more keen over time. For Leontine, it was human nature. For some reason she understood why people did the things they did, said what they said, even thought what they thought. Not that all were the same. Quite the contrary. There were certainly some underlying similarities amongst humans, assuming their faculties were largely intact, but as various as they were, still Leontine could understand. Had she communicated this understanding to those around her, she may have found herself well liked. It is a yearning in us all, the wish to be understood. But she did not. She observed and understood in silence. Leontine felt compassion for her struggling earthly companions and did not judge. She even felt kindly in nearly every circumstance. But life had been ruthless with her, betraying and unfathomable. As stolid as she appeared the truth was something more fragile. Uncertain. She was overcome by wariness and waited always for another shoe to drop and so she mostly remained silent and often appeared withdrawn. Perhaps it was the age of her young escort or his premature wisdom that put her at ease. She found she enjoyed hearing his thoughts and was uncensored in sharing her own.

As they walked beside the horse and wagon, Leontine learned that Patrick was born in St. Louis and that his mother died in childbirth. As a result his father studied hard to become a physician and eventually opened a small office as a general practitioner in Santa Barbara, California, far from the painful memories of the city that had claimed his bride. Leontine wondered if her own life would have been better had her mother perished during the birth of her stillborn sister rather than lingering in anguish and poor health for several more years. When her mother finally succumbed, Leontine and her father were worn out from the care of her, and if truth were told, the release from the servitude of her mother's ill health and depression outweighed the grief of her loss.

Although it was as warm as a day in summer now, March had seen weeks of soaking rain and the tiny troupe had to pick their way carefully through overgrown areas still boggy from the spring showers as they neared the oceanfront. The dirt path grew increasingly soggy and uneven and Leontine was grateful for the assistance of young Patrick. She marveled at his attention to their surroundings and his foresight and planning as they moved along. When the pair got to Montecito Street they headed east and, rather than simply use the service entrance a half block away, Leontine continued on to Chapala Street in order to treat Patrick to the more aesthetic entrance used by those arriving from the Southern Pacific railway station behind the hotel. Leontine urged the reluctant Otis over the railroad tracks and a concrete bridge that crossed once again over Mission Creek, and then finally approached the side entrance to the magnificent Potter Hotel. She coaxed Otis to stand and tied his reins to a hitching post at the side of a service path that led to the kitchens from the train station. Patrick ordered Tesla to "stay", which the dog seemed willing enough to do. He curled into a circle in the shade under the wagon in preparation for a nap, though his eyes tracked Patrick's every move until the boy was out of sight.

Leontine watched his young face as they passed between substantial block sandstone gateposts and underneath tall block lettering adorned in wrought iron that proudly proclaimed: "THE POTTER" Patrick's expression did not disappoint. He could hardly believe where he was. Several of his fellow grade-schoolers had been inside. Milo Potter was a generous man and eager to please the community that served his distinguished clientele with such excellence. Nearly ten percent of the population of Santa Barbara was employed at the massive concern in one capacity or another and, as long as the privilege was not abused, the odd family member was allowed to deliver an important message or some such endeavor and thereby catch a glimpse of the very, very good life.

Mr. Potter was also careful to put local businessmen to use. While his grand hotel required many goods and services by the trainload – a need fulfilled by a rail spur to the rear of the hotel – so, too, did he frequent the businesses of Santa Barbara on a daily basis. Local fruits and vegetables, fish, fowl and diary goods flowed through the kitchen in endless quantity. Though he employed a physician on the premises he would occasionally call on Patrick's father if there was need for another. Nevertheless, Patrick so far had seen only the opulent landscaping from the Boulevard where the oceanfront hotel seemed miles away across spacious lawns, flowerbeds and walkways.

The broad doors the pair entered led directly into the kitchens. At any given moment there could be as many as one hundred waitresses, forty dishwashers, twenty busboys and as many cooks, in addition to head chefs and even private chefs that accompanied their wealthy employers. The noise was stunning. At this early afternoon hour all in the kitchen were engaged in feverish preparation of the elaborate menu items that would tantalize and satiate the esteemed guests dining at the Potter that evening. Two boys tended the spit jacks, upon which slowly spun a dozen turkeys over open flame. Several dozens of lobsters wriggled in a squirming pile in a giant sink, ignorant of an enormous tin of water being brought to a boil nearby. The cooks at the bread ovens were in continuous motion generating a veritable mountain of bread that would be entirely consumed by evening's end. Another handful of cooks peeled and chopped and prepped and piled endless wooden cases of fresh fruits and vegetables, some having been plucked from the Potter's own gardens not an hour before. Meats and cheeses, cakes and pies, and everyone barking orders with seemingly no one free to follow them. There was nothing else like it.

Leontine guided Patrick to a relatively calm position near the door, telling him she would just be a moment. She made quick work of finding the person she wanted; a young Mexican man who wore a jacket indicating his station as upper hotel management. Leontine related the whereabouts of the delivery out on the walkway and the young man sent others to the task of retrieving the goods.

Leontine's French grandfather, like countless other European men who found themselves in this bucolic setting on the central coast of California some hundred years prior, had taken a Mexican girl as his bride. Many, if not most, of these black-eyed beauties were by then several generations descended from Mexican landowners who came to eventually refer to themselves only as "Californios," the umbilical cord to Mexico City long ago severed. Family histories wove in and out, more spider web than tree, and nearly all the Mexican families in Santa Barbara could count themselves related to the once powerful Carrillo, De la Guerra, Cota or Ortega families. Leontine could trace her Ortega roots to the founding of the city as a Spanish fort in 1782. Her great, great, great grandfather, José Francisco Ortega, had been the first comandante of the presidio and was himself married to a Carrillo. At one point this early Ortega bloodline joined with that of the Ordaz family, the result of a coupling between a blushing Ortega girl and a frisky Franciscan, Father Blas Ordaz at Mission Santa Ines. This ancient union was currently expressed in the person of her cousin, Danny, who had impressed his way into this position of responsibility and now bossed the staff into heading out to the delivery wagon.

Leontine and Danny then approached Patrick watching the activity around him with wide-eyed interest from his spot by the door.

"This is my cousin Danny. Danny, Patrick," Leontine told them. "Patrick came to my rescue earlier today."

Danny bowed low and extended his hand. Patrick had not had overly many opportunities to shake hands and hoped he was doing it well. Danny stood straighter, glanced over each shoulder, then bent to whisper something to Patrick conspiratorially.

"Would you like to see the dining hall?"

Although Leontine had seen nearly all the public areas of the hotel, she followed after the two anticipating Patrick's reaction and feeling some reflection of the wonder she had experienced herself the first time she walked through the luxurious space. She had spent plenty of time in the company of a dozen children Patrick's age, but none had made her feel anything, really, and so she marveled at the sense of pleasure she felt at the idea of seeing this young boy smile again.

Chapter 2

In this month of April 1908, the Great White Fleet was close to completion of the first leg of a journey circumnavigating the globe by order of President Theodore Roosevelt, on a mission to impress all on the planet with the awesome might and great good will of the United States Navy. The sixteen battleships in the fleet did, in fact, have their hulls painted white, thus signaling to other vessels that this voyage was a peaceful one. All of the battleships were named for various states in the union with the exception of the USS *Kearsage*, originally launched in 1898 and named for a mountain in New Hampshire. The flagship, the four hundred fifty-six foot USS *Connecticut*, boasted sixty-six massive guns of varying size and four submerged torpedo tubes. All this while managing to provide room enough for more than eight hundred crewmen, supplies, ammunition and the two thousand tons of coal required to fuel her on to the next destination.

The fleet had been deployed from Hampton Roads, Virginia in December of 1907 and had since traveled around all of South America, harboring in ports in Trinidad, Brazil, Chile, Peru, and many others countries along the way. The battleships traveled in the company of the fleet auxiliary ships, which included two store ships, a repair ship, a coal tender and a hospital ship.

This massive flotilla was now gathering in San Diego and the military officers were in the throes of hurried reorganization in order to cope with the removal of Rear Admiral Robley D. Evans. Suffering with symptoms of rheumatic gout for much of the deployment, Evans finally succumbed to the pain in Magdalena Bay, Baja California. The *Connecticut* split off in advance of the fleet for the two-day voyage to deliver the ailing Rear Admiral to San Diego from whence he could be transported to a health sanatorium in Paso Robles by rail. Captain John Adams had gradually assumed many of the Rear Admiral's duties as the encroaching illness took an increasing toll on his ability to command.

Adams, a robust man of forty-two years, well over six feet in height with a square jaw and sharp eyes, proved an able commander of the eight ships in his squadron. Born in Philadelphia, his family, friends and professors had always suspected his charismatic charm would propel him toward success in whatever path he chose. The military proved to be the perfect arena in which to showcase his talents. Here in San Diego however, the fleet was to welcome Rear Admiral Percifal Haines, who would see this part of the excursion through to San Francisco. It rankled Captain Adams. He had felt capable in the elevated position of power. More than capable, completely at ease, with not only the power but also the admiration the position garnered from rank and file crewmen. In truth he had no wish to relinquish command, especially to the condescending bureaucrat Haines who tended toward pudginess and whose thin, reedy voice failed to motivate or inspire.

That Captain Adams shared a name with no less than two former United States presidents was a fact not lost on him. Military men often aspired to the position of Commander in Chief and Adams had admitted, if only to himself, that it was a role he could see himself filling. He had the confidence and charisma to carry the thing off, too. Many had said so and though he would laugh it off with feigned humility he did all he could to see that the observation spread as far as possible.

There were further complications at this point in the expedition, however. The entire trek had been a protracted series of ostentatious display and pageantry and President Roosevelt intended to finish this first leg of the journey with a bang. Lilly White, the social-climbing daughter of Senator Deacon "Duke" White from the great state of Mississippi, had been appointed by the State Department as "hostess" for the fleet, that she might put a pretty face on these gargantuan weapons of war. She had met with some of the ships the preceding year in various seaports on the east coast as they each made their way to Hampton Roads for the launch of the fleet. With fair-haired curls, ice blue eyes, trim waist and ample bosom, and a sparkling banter delivered with the honeyed drawl depicting her southern origins, Lilly exalted in this unparalleled opportunity as hostess to scout a very broad horizon for what she envisioned as a suitable mate - someone handsome and powerful and, hopefully, at least a little bit kind. Though Captain Adams had a wife and, sadly, a severely retarded teen-aged son, on one champagne-soaked night in North Carolina the senator's daughter had professed a strong attraction to the Captain and he had not done all he could to dissuade her ardor. Since that night, whenever he learned Lilly White was to characterize the fleet in city-wide revelry, Captain Adams had engaged in a delicate balancing act, hoping her attraction could benefit him somehow with her powerful father, while simultaneously keeping her at arm's length to protect her reputation and, more importantly, his own. For him it was not difficult to gain the admiration and desire of a woman, but it was tricky to keep the pitch fevered with little or no chance of consummation at the end. Nevertheless, he had managed to do just that thus far.

But now he had learned Lilly White was to travel with them on board the *Connecticut* to provide the public with the sailors' experience from their point of view as they docked in the various seaports of southern California. She would be accompanied by her Aunt Anne, a somewhat rummy old dame whose eyes twinkled a bit too brightly at the able-bodied seamen that would surround her onboard the ship. Not a bad arrangement on the face of things, but they were scheduled to dock in Santa Barbara, the residing place of his wife and son. This promised to be a balancing act indeed.

And there was something else, something of even greater significance given his ultimate aspiration. There are three things a man needs plenty of if he has his eye on a prize as big as ruler of the free world: power, influence and, above all, money. Toward that end he had engineered a surreptitious, if somewhat hurried, meeting with one Steven Magness of the Allied Steel Company. He had only twenty minutes until his presence was required for the pomp and ceremony of welcoming Rear Admiral Haines and the lovely Lilly White and her libidinous chaperone on board his vessel.

Captain Adams was in possession of important documentation passed to him by the ailing Rear Admiral Evans just prior to his departure by train for the health sanatorium in Paso Robles, along with instruction that they be delivered in San Francisco only to Senator White himself. In his capacity as head of the Appropriations Committee of the United States Congress in Washington, D.C., Senator White would be more than interested to learn that the report bore clear evidence of malfeasance and fraud in grand scale by Allied Steel as a major supplier of steel for the intercontinental railroads. The company was now under consideration as a provider for the upgrading and expansion of the naval fleet, a consideration that would undoubtedly evaporate if the content of the report proved true; that substandard materials and accelerated production schedules had resulted in product failures that could be linked to numerous rail accidents and the death of over two dozen railway workers and innocent passengers. Several noted scientists had attached their names to the damning evidence.

Captain Adams situated himself at a table in the lounge of the Coronado del Mar Hotel and waited for Magness to show up wondering how best to use these documents to further his march to the White House. Simple extortion was repugnant to him, but he felt certain he could find a way to turn the paper into gold. He looked at his timepiece, then stared impatiently at the door.

Chapter 3

Leontine saved the best for last. Danny had treated his cousin and her appreciative companion to several of the most enthralling stations at the Potter Hotel. The dining hall was already set for dinner. Danny led the way up a back staircase that ended at a balcony extending over the wide doors to the kitchen where live music would mask the sounds from the preparations inside and the endless comings and goings of the wait staff. From that vantage point the marvel of so many dozens of tables adorned in white linen and set with porcelain and silver, each piece emblazoned with the image of a bell bearing the name, "The Potter", was a wonder to behold. Gleaming wood flooring and the deep richness of oak furniture lent a sense of comfort to the giant room with its elaborately ornamented ceiling exhibiting artful paint, gilding and hundreds of glimmering lights.

As overwhelming as the dining hall was, the grand entry hall was even more spectacular. The lighted ceiling seemed impossibly high and the pillars and archways that drew patrons inside to the opulent receiving desks could be viewed from a balcony that rimmed the entire area. Affluent visitors from all over the United States and abroad moved about the sumptuous appointments with smiles and soft voices as they absorbed the luxury and beauty provided by Milo Potter and the hundreds he employed. Many came for the entire "season", soaking up the warm sun on the south-facing coast of California while relatives and co-workers back east or in the mid-west shoveled their way through snow and freezing temperatures from November often well into March.

At the end opposite the majestic entry was a doorway leading into the grand ballroom. Patrick was allowed to step inside the room, and though empty at the moment, it only served to make the expansive maple floor seem even more vast. He would have loved to run and jump and spin and slide on the glistening floor in an effort to somehow touch the emptiness of the space with a feeling of boundlessness or even flight. He felt smaller than he ever had and at the same time able to fill the room with his own excitement.

The tiny group had then taken the stairs to the first floor located beneath that of the main entry. They walked the length of a corridor that passed by more corridors leading to laundry and linen rooms, storage rooms for wine, groceries and furnishings, a tailor, a barber and carpentry room and terminating at the incredible game rooms. There, Patrick saw the wealthy patrons of the hotel playing at billiards and shuffleboard and trying their hand on the two-lane Brunswick bowling alley. Two boys, not much older than Patrick, acted as pin setters, replacing the bowling pins in their triangular arrangement once some enthusiastic guest had done his best to knock them all down. Amongst billiard tables and card tables and tables situated around and about apparently for their own sake, Danny and Leontine encouraged Patrick to feel the heft of a cue stick or test the slickness of the shuffleboard surface with a "biscuit" and even to feel the surprising weight of a bowling ball. To his delight they poked their heads into a separate room devoted entirely to ping pong and though he ducked his head in shy response when the sweating young men deep into a game waved their paddles in greeting, he was at the same time deeply thrilled.

Patrick had never been in an elevator before, and Danny, pretending he had missed his intended floor, treated Patrick to several trips all the way up to the fifth floor and back down until finally returning to the main floor where they abandoned the elevator car, walked across the lobby and stepped out onto the sun porch. Comfortable wooden rocking chairs were strewn about the spacious deck that overlooked the Pacific Ocean, and more than a few guests were taking advantage of the sunny day. Just beyond the sun porch was the sun parlor, where those of a more delicate nature could enjoy the warmth of the sun through glass windows, protected from ocean breezes that could at times be quite chilly.

But now they were heading toward what Leontine suspected would be the high point of the tour. Danny explained he had business on an upper floor, and Leontine said she and Patrick would find their own way back to the kitchen after they made one more stop and she exchanged a wink with her cousin. Danny deposited Leontine and Patrick on the first floor once more, said his good-byes, and then disappeared behind the sliding doors of the elevator. Leontine and Patrick headed down the hallway in the direction of the game rooms they had visited earlier, but this time they paused in front of the door leading into Mahesy's Art & Fur Store, known widely as the Curio Shop.

As Leontine had suspected he might, Patrick dove into the shop and immediately lost himself in the art and oddities crammed into every nook and corner of the store. It was impossible not to first notice a row of genuine bear skin rugs laid out and overlapping on the floor, their massive paws, claws and all, draped over the shoulder of the next bear in line so that their giant snarling heads lay side-by-side like a congenial, yet terrifying, chorus line. Most were a deep brownish-black but there were two polar-bear skins as well that were a most astonishing sight. Along the wall above the bear skin rugs was situated a long, gleaming pole made of brass which held ornamented silk kimonos from Japan, beaded and adorned saris from India, as well as some uncommon and boldly-styled fashions from New York and Chicago. Facing the garments on the opposing wall was an elaborately adorned vanity with an attendant velvet-covered stool. Here, a woman could look into the attached gilded mirror and hold intricately crafted jewels of every type and origin against her face or body in order to determine whether or not she could live without them.

Around the entire circumference of the store between the ceiling and the clothing and glass display cases filled with oddities and art from far and wide, hung the skins of more exotic animals; tiger, cheetah, zebra and onyx. Like the bear rugs, some of the larger cat skins still had their fearsome heads attached. And there were many more heads of elk, ram and moose, all mounted in such a way that their antlers intertwined yet did not touch.

Leontine watched carefully as Patrick inspected the items, already having decided that she would reward his care of her with some token as a souvenir of his exciting visit. She was fairly certain she would know the thing when she saw it and she was not mistaken. Resting on a table surrounded by sealing wax displays from Great Britain and iron candlesticks from Mexico, sat a leather encased tool kit. When Patrick unsnapped a leather strap and opened the kit, he found tiny perfect tools including a wood handled screwdriver, pick and even a small tack hammer, each intricately arranged in fabric pouches. Separate sleeves held a compass, fishing line and a flint stone for starting fires. Patrick spent quite a bit of time with the item and when he reluctantly set it down and turned his attention to a display of carvings made of ivory, she scooped it up and silently communicated to the clerk that she would be making a purchase.

Chapter 4

Rear Admiral Haines' feet hurt. He was exhausted from his inspection of the ship and its complement of crewmen and he gratefully lowered himself into the leather chair in his shipboard office knowing he had some unpleasant conversations ahead of him. He felt a flash of annoyance that his feet did not comfortably reach the floor causing him to slouch in the chair. He would have to procure a footrest. He rubbed his puffy eyes for a moment, then picked up his reading glasses from the desktop and began rearranging papers and supplies to suit his own preference. He had requested immediate consultation with Captain Adams and also the bothersome Lilly White and her aunt and knew they would appear in short order.

The Captain was the first to arrive. Adams saluted his commanding officer upon entering the room and stopped himself from curling his lip at the flaccid salute with which the Rear Admiral responded. Admiral Haines ordered the younger man to stand at ease. If Adams relaxed at all it was imperceptible. Haines was immune to this military posturing. Being one of four sons of a military father, all engaged in military careers, he had been provided with more than a lifetime of it. Haines was second born, a poor second act to the glory that had been his elder brother who had distinguished himself so dazzlingly in the Spanish American war. This brother now enjoyed an advisory post, kept on retainer by the United States congressional body, to inform and educate politicians who had sudden and immediate need to understand the ways of war lords, military strategy or government contract suppliers. Military life did not come naturally to Percifal who had always been sedentary and bookish. His rise through the ranks was a product of the accident of his birth into such a celebrated military family and strict adherence to regulation rather than ambition or drive for distinction. He seemed absent of the competitiveness that drove his siblings and fellow officers in an endless pursuit of advancement. In fact, he viewed these motivations as weakness.

Haines got right to the point. Locking eyes with Captain Adams he said, "I understand you are in possession of some documents intended for Senator White."

Adams willed his facial muscles to freeze. If Haines relieved him of his duty to the Senator it could impede the negotiations begun with Steven Magness. "Yes, Sir," he replied.

"Deliver them personally to this office."

"Sir." Adams saluted, then spun on his heel to leave the room. There was nothing for it. But it didn't necessarily change anything. The power-driven young Captain wondered, and not for the first time, why Rear Admiral Evans entrusted him with the documents in the first place. Either his confidence in the Captain surpassed what he felt for the Rear Admiral, or he had wanted to benefit Adams in some way - one that was not entirely apparent to him at the moment - or perhaps even to protect himself from some unknown reprisal. Quite possibly the Captain would never know what was true. As he reached for the door it was pushed open from the other side by Lilly White, trailed by her aunt who carried an open parasol, though she had been indoors for hours.

Lilly's eyelashes went to work. She blushed prettily and expressed her delight at seeing the Captain again, conscious and intentional of how one's posture presented one's décolletage. Aunt Anne all but rolled her eyes. She knew the connivings of her niece better than anyone, and though she could certainly understand the attraction to this masculine Captain, Anne knew also that there were plenty of fish in just about any sea — and the Navy went double for that. She saw no reason for her niece to waste time on a married man, no matter his rank and privilege. Captain Adams returned the attention lavishly, directing his compliments to both women. Balancing.

When Adams had closed the door behind him Rear Admiral Haines cleared his throat to gain the attention of the females. Lilly gushed at the Rear Admiral immediately.

"This is the high point of my life! I can't wait to start sailing!"

"Sit down," the Admiral ordered.

The flush on her face was genuine. However appealing she found Captain Adams and his aspirations, there was no denying the stimulation of treading water in a sea of so much manhood. Rear Admiral Haines had no use for women, yet he tried to keep the disdain he felt for that gender in check as he began to rein in the exuberance of this young woman in his charge. Nothing good ever came from exuberance. Her attraction to the Captain was undisguised and Haines became determined to quash it for no other reason than peevishness. The Captain annoyed him with his confidence and charm and the Rear Admiral's resentment for the sideshow this vapid girl represented in the presence of his mighty fleet annoyed him even more.

Though Percifal's harsh and judgmental father was at that moment warming a seat cushion at a veterans' retirement home in Pennsylvania, he was simultaneously folded into a dark hole inside Haines' own heart and both men lashed out with a harshness not equal to the situation at hand.

"You will receive your itinerary daily at oh-six-thirty in this office. Crew interaction is limited to your assigned detail. No exceptions."

Lilly, though inwardly crestfallen, was not accustomed to having her personal desires thwarted and her chin stuck out defiantly. It was her aunt who responded, however.

"Am I to understand you mean six o'clock in the morning?" she attempted to clarify.

"O-six-thirty. Dismissed."

He turned his attention to some files on his desk to encourage the hasty retreat of the females. Lilly, aghast, turned an incredulous face to her chaperone and folded her arms across her chest. Aunt Anne shook her head almost imperceptibly and waited for privacy to communicate to her niece that there were ways around everything, military protocol included.

* * *

Later that night, Haines, still at his desk, held in his hands the documents delivered by Captain Adams. So…it was true: Rear Admiral Haines had learned of the papers from Kurt Gunn, President of Amalgamated Incorporated in San Francisco. Gunn himself had prepared the report, his desire to bring the fraud and theft perpetrated by Allied Steel to the attention of the Chief of Naval Operations - perhaps even the Secretary of the Navy - as would have been the case had naval doctrine and protocol been observed. The fact that regulation was skirted caused bitterness and bile to rise in the Rear Admiral's throat. He well knew what was happening and why. It was irksome, the continuing flow of posing and profiteering miscreants that rose in the ranks of the military, so often shooting past him like errant asteroids around a fixed and steady sun. Information like this should have been delivered into the hands of the highest-ranking officer and immediately dispatched by carrier. Had that occurred there may well have been corrective actions already in play. If not for the businessman Gunn, Rear Admiral Haines may well have been kept in the dark all along for reasons that could only be interpreted as "political". He spat the word in his mind. Politics were the enemy of discipline. A siren's song that had dashed many a military career to ruins against the cliffs of popular opinion. Disgusting.

Chapter 5

When Leontine returned to the Birabent Market, she found her Uncle Remi preparing to lock up for the day. Remi Birabent was her father's older brother; a pleasant man, pleasant looking with a pleasing temperament. His features were dominated by a rather large mustache, one that Leontine often offered to trim up for him, though he had, so far, each time declined. He had a thick head of hair and steady brown eyes that somehow seemed to encourage others to confide in him that which they no doubt had intended to keep to themselves. He said little of himself, however, and though many in the town of Santa Barbara no doubt believed they knew him well, only a very few actually did. Remi's heart was heavy with the death of his younger brother, Francois, Leontine's father, and the heartache left him somber and somewhat removed.

Nearly three years earlier, Francois, along with Leontine's fiancé, Vincent Barón, had left the Birabent Market with a delivery bound for Mattei's Tavern in the Santa Ynez valley. They headed off over the San Marcos Pass and then, some ten hours after their departure, the horses, pulling the fully loaded wagon and the body of Francois Birabent, found their own way to Cold Spring Tavern near the top of the pass. There was no evidence of foul play and no clue what had become of Birabent's soon-to-be son-in-law. The death had been declared "from natural causes" though there was nothing natural about the situation. Leontine combed every inch of the pass in the two years that followed but turned up nothing that could explain what had ended the life of her father or what had become of the man she was to marry. She never thought the day would come, but she had finally lost hope of ever knowing what truly happened the day she was left suddenly and forever on her own.

Remi did not attempt to discourage Leontine from her relentless and dispiriting investigation into the tragedy, nor did he really help. He had spent the first two and a half decades of his adult life as a janitor, most recently at St. Francis Hospital on the northeast corner of town. He willingly left that employ and donned the floor-length apron of a shopkeeper, stepping into his brother's life without a moment of hesitation. A blanket of sorrow wrapped around Remi leaving him steeped in empathy for the trials of humanity. He listened to the troubles and joys of their daily customers and kept a watchful eye on Leontine, hoping against hope that one day they would both be able to truly put it all behind and look with some measure of eagerness into the future. That time had not yet come.

"A girl came by to see the room," Remi informed Leontine, as he handed over the receipts and order tickets from the day's endeavors.

Leontine had lived in the apartments above the store since she was a child. The front door was at street level next to the open storefront and a flight of stairs led to an open entrance to the apartment. A doorbell, that made a sound big enough to carry upstairs when its handle was twisted, was affixed below a glass panel surrounded by colored glass ornamentation. The double doors of the market opened onto State Street and Leontine and Remi would carry cartons draped with linen towels to the sidewalk each morning and load them with tempting displays of the fresh foods, juices, cooking oils, spices, supplies and sundry items that could be found in ample quantity inside. They were also mindful to rotate items neatly stacked in the window displays, placed carefully between the glass of the window and the lace curtains inside, so that printed labels would not fade. The store was clean and orderly with large wooden bins holding fresh fruits and vegetables and installed with casters on the legs so they could be easily moved about. A large, twenty pound hanging produce scale was situated above the bins, and on either side of it, hanging on similar hooks, could usually be found three or four spreading bunches of ripening bananas often surpassing three feet in length.

The upstairs apartment where Leontine lived contained a comfortable living room with airy windows overlooking the bustling activity on State Street below, a dining room, kitchen, bathroom and sun porch and four bedrooms down the length of a hallway. Leontine's parents always took in a boarder or two to help with paying the bills and to also provide added companionship for their only child. Not that she ever availed herself of the company. Her well-meaning parents did not realize that the boarders were adults who, if they wanted children, would probably have had some.

As her uncle's news registered Leontine's lips became a line. She was loath to give up her solitude. No one dared question it for a stretch of time, but some unspoken and generalized agreement had apparently been reached that her grieving time was up and she had best open her door at least to some family if not friends.

"Who is she?" Leontine pretended to wonder, already resolute that any application would be denied.

"She'll be back. She's been here twice already," her uncle said.

Leontine sighed.

"Give her a chance. She's nice."

Barely an hour later Leontine responded to the grinding chime of the doorbell. She headed down the stairs as she smoothed the fitted front of her charcoal-colored gored skirt and pulled at the sleeves of the much cooler linen shirt she had changed into, dyed a golden sunflower yellow with embroidered embellishments at the collar and sleeves. Leontine had a weakness for fashion and allowed herself several new garments each year. Her dressmaker, Victoria Ramirez, prided herself in stocking the most current and stylish patterns and her work was exquisite, far superior to the ready-made fare available at Trenwith's, Walton's Department Store or even Rochester Clothing. She looked through the glass panel of the front door to get a first glimpse of the girl. After rapping on the door however, the caller had turned her back to it in order to observe the sunny stream of humanity passing by on State Street. From the back she appeared youthful and though well groomed, her course wool skirt and limp cotton shirtwaist suggested a modest station in life. Her wavy, reddish-brown hair was swept up and gathered in a loose knot at the top of her head and she twisted a broad brimmed hat in her hands as she looked at the businesses across the street; Santa Barbara Wholesale

Liquor, Angelo Miratti's saloon, Vogel Cigars and of course the Tally Ho, among others. At the sound of the door opening behind her, the young woman spun to face what she hoped would become her new landlord. She thrust out a hand immediately, offering her name and a greeting. Leontine took her hand lightly, recoiling inwardly and ever so slightly at the girl's cheerful name, Daisy Merrie. She had sparkling green eyes, freckles and dimples that matched the name precisely, and when she smiled she revealed an appealing little space between her two front teeth. Young Daisy was unable to stop her eyes from sweeping over and around Leontine in an effort to get a glimpse of the place. Obligingly, Leontine pulled the door more fully open and motioned for Daisy to precede her up the stairs.

The space above the Birabent Market had been designed as a family home intending to serve whoever was making a go of the retail space below at any given time. The entry was open to the main living space on the left that included the large windows overlooking State Street. The positioning of the furniture belied time spent by Leontine in just that endeavor. Daisy took in the comfortable warmth of the room. Though inviting, the dark wood and upholstered furniture gave the tidy place a somewhat masculine air. A mantle had been attached to the exterior wall and would have looked great with a fireplace, but none had been installed. Instead it surrounded an iron grate that held an arrangement of foliage and dried flowers. The shelf of the mantle supported items presumably reflective of some aspect of its owner, as mantle shelves often will. There was a brass bell the size of a grown man's fist, a delicate fluted vase holding a sparse bouquet of long-dead flowers and a wooden picture frame lying flat on its face, sharing its content only with the mantle shelf it rested on.

A center coffee table was already arranged with tea and biscuits and Leontine motioned once more, guiding Daisy to seat herself on the loveseat near the refreshments. Daisy actually wished she could just poke around the place on her own but hopefully there would be plenty of time for that. She felt too nervous to sit but did not want to make her hostess uncomfortable, so she perched on the edge of the loveseat, laid her hat on the cushion beside her and smiled brightly at Leontine who poured a cup of tea for each of them and then sat facing Daisy in a wooden rocker that could easily be turned to face the window or the room's interior, whichever suited.

Leontine began, "How long have you been in Santa Barbara?"

Daisy set down her tea. She didn't want to have to think about whether she was holding it, sipping it, doing it right. She asked, "What time is it now?"

"My heavens, have you only come in today? How did you know about the room?"

"The train came in last night but I haven't slept yet so it seems like one very long day."

"I can imagine."

Leontine sipped her tea and watched the girl for a moment. Daisy openly gazed around the room waiting for the next question.

"I love this place," Daisy remarked, after several moments of perusal.

"So do I."

And Leontine decided just that quickly that Daisy would become her tenant. Without ever acknowledging her own criteria for a decision, Daisy had inadvertently stumbled onto what was possibly the only thing that truly mattered to Leontine. If Daisy loved the place any area of concern would sort itself out naturally. Besides, there was something about this girl - a twinkle or a sparkle that made her eye shine in something that probably meant mischief. Rather than being put off by the twinkle Leontine nearly formed the thought that she wouldn't mind a spark of her own if she could find a way to it.

She asked, "What kind of work will you be looking for? I'm sorry, I assume you will be working."

Daisy tilted her head, unable in that moment to envision a life that did not include work. Was there such a thing?

"I already got a job," she said. "I'm a newspaperman – a journalist. Newspapers are always crawling with people so I went to them all last night."

"How fortunate someone was hiring a writer."

"No one was. I can set type though so that got me in at the *Daily News*. I plan to do some stories on my own – you know – show them what I can do. I wrote for a paper in San Francisco. Just after the fire."

Daisy couldn't help but sit a little straighter when she said the words. The earthquake and devastating fire in San Francisco two years earlier had dominated newspapers all across the continent for many months. Compared with San Francisco, Santa Barbara was a sleepy seaside village, so it was no doubt true, up to a point, that experience in that arena might yield an elevated level of skill.

"Would you like to see your room?" Leontine asked, as she set down her tea.

Daisy smiled and let out the breath she didn't know she was holding. "I most certainly would."

Another hour later Leontine was preparing dinner for herself and her new boarder. She had purchased a beautiful mackerel from Larco's and snitched some greens and a large whipping potato from the bins downstairs earlier in the day. As she opened the tin of milk to mix into the mashed up potato she could hear Daisy down the hall putting away her scant belongings and banging around in cupboards as she apparently decided where things should go. Leontine found the sounds comforting and thought perhaps people were right. Maybe it was time to lift her eyes and gaze a bit farther afield. As she stood at the sink Leontine heard the sound of the doorbell below. She lifted the iron skillet from the stove top to keep the fish from burning, wiped her hands on her apron and hurried downstairs to the door. She opened it to reveal young Patrick, solemnly staring at his shoes. He held the leather tool kit to his chest in the crook of one arm, Tesla panting at his feet. A smile did not seem in order. Something was amiss.

"Patrick?" Leontine gently probed.

Without looking directly at Leontine, Patrick extended the tool kit in her direction. He told her, "My dad says I have to give it back."

Leontine took the kit and stood aside, reaching her hand behind Patrick's shoulder to gently guide him inside. Tesla paused, one paw over the threshold as if waiting for his own invitation. Leontine gave him a slight nod and he immediately scooted past them and sprinted up the stairs.

"But why?" Leontine asked, as she followed after the young boy. "Did you explain how you helped me? Did you tell him about the Potter visit?" She was at a loss to understand.

Once inside the apartment Tesla stuck close to Patrick, actually sitting on the boy's foot as they stood in the hall just inside the doorway. Patrick wiped his nose with his hand. One day Leontine would have a word with him about that.

"I was supposed to be in school." He looked into her eyes at last with something like a plea for understanding.

And Leontine did understand. What did a classroom have to offer a child like this? He would be bored to madness. And yet, how could his father allow his young son to roam the streets like a wild coyote, especially with no mother at home to keep track of his wanderings? How very troublesome for both.

"I'll keep it for you for now, but would you mind if I talk to your father about it?"

Patrick said, "You're a grown up. You can do whatever you want."

"If only that were true. Come on, there's someone I want you to meet." And they headed down the hallway to find Daisy.

Chapter 6

The following morning the Great White Fleet was preparing to sail
to Los Angeles. The sixteen battleships would scatter, docking in Long
Beach, Redondo Beach, Santa Monica and San Pedro. Rear Admiral
Haines would never have admitted to himself that he took pleasure in
keeping Captain Adams aboard the flagship, thereby rendering him
second-in-command for the duration. Had he transferred him to another
ship the Captain would have ruled that one dominion at least. As it was,
he was forced into the Rear Admiral's diminutive shadow. Haines would
break this stallion and bring him into the corral to serve – as was only right.

It was approaching six-forty when Lilly White and her grumpy
and sleep-deprived aunt arrived at his office. The women took chairs
facing the Rear Admiral, Anne leaning gratefully into the back of the
seat. Haines pushed a single sheet of paper across his desk for the young
woman to pick up. She did so tentatively, then began to read. Her eyes
scanned the bullet-point list and though she did not know it, her head
rotated back and forth, clearly communicating the word "no" to those
around her.

"I – we – were to have luncheon at the Van Nuys Hotel with Captain
Adams," Lilly said, "and I believe there is a soiree planned in Pasadena. I
don't see them here."

"Captain Adams is remaining aboard the vessel. Your day is full and
you will be prompt in future. Your detail is standing by. You are cleared
to go ashore."

And that was that.

Lilly's brow clouded. This was not how she had envisioned this leg of the journey she had so fervently anticipated. The previous year on the east coast had been grand: dancing, parties, speeches, the adoration of men and women alike. The flirtatious bantering she had begun with Captain Adams in North Carolina needed care and feeding if she was to convince him of her suitability as someone who could share his ride into the halls of power and prestige. How would she accomplish that if this silly puffed-up sailor stood between her and her prize? She turned to her aunt, hoping for a champion, but Anne's eyelids had not come apart the last time she blinked and her chin was sinking dangerously close to her chest. No help would come from that quarter.

"I am not one of your crewmen to be commanded about. I fear you overstep your bounds Admiral Haines." Clearly he was not nearly as impressed as he should be with her position as the daughter of Duke White.

"I command everyone in this fleet. I would as soon put you ashore to find your own way for the remainder of the mission and look only for a reason to do so. You will find the chain of command stops at this desk where your activities are concerned. You are dismissed."

Haines removed his attention from the girl and did not look up as she prodded her aunt and stormed from the room. He was unaware of the smirk that crept onto his face as the door shut between them.

Chapter 7

Nicholas Denman allowed himself two fingers of whiskey in an effort to recover from an exceedingly trying day. His classes in medical school had not prepared him for the psychological aspect of practicing medicine – and how could they possibly? Nicholas was a thoughtful and soft-spoken man, not overly tall or short or slender or wide. Nor was he verbose. He tended to choose his words carefully and was direct but gentle in his communication, no doubt the result of being forced to deliver unwelcome news to his patients on so many occasions. For days he had been dealing with the aftermath of an unconscionable criminal who had passed through Santa Barbara the week before selling patent medicine to an unsuspecting public, promising a cure for ailments as diverse as obesity, arthritis and diabetes. Several of the citizenry had ended up at the Cottage Hospital. Thankfully, none had died. One such victim was none other than the wife of Captain John Adams who had subjected her son to the cure, hoping to free him from the devastating betrayal of his own anatomy. The boy was a victim of Down's Syndrome, Mongoloidism. His devoted mother knew better than to hope a ten-dollar vial of foul smelling fluid could repair the damage done by his chromosomes and so she was now awash in guilt and remorse.

"His father is coming in with the fleet," she said. "He demands that I keep his son out of sight."

The steel of her eye communicated what her words did not; she had no deep fondness for her husband. Nicholas felt sympathy for the woman mixed with horror that she would allow herself to be taken in by the transparent sham of a snake oil salesman. He had been looking forward to the arrival of the fleet, as had most in town, and found that the experience with Mrs. Adams dampened his anticipation. If this hard-hearted father was one of the men in charge he had no wish to participate in his glorification.

Nicholas downed the liquor in one motion and wiped his mouth with his sleeve. At any moment the piano teacher would show up at his door. Just when he thought he had managed to create some order in the luckless life of his tiny family, here she was to insert herself and disrupt and create tension between himself and his son. He traipsed from room to room in his small two bedroom cottage on De La Vina Street, making certain the place seemed in order. He then looked out the kitchen window into the back yard to check on Patrick who was, as usual, making something. He had gathered some small bushy branches from somewhere and appeared to be stripping them of their leaves. It would be interesting to see what became of the raw materials. He had asked Patrick to wait outside until his conversation with the fainting piano teacher was done. In a short time there came the expected knock. He wrestled his annoyance to the ground, planted a smile on his face and opened the door.

Leontine was momentarily stunned. For some reason she had not been expecting a man so young. He was a physician after all, and everyone she had ever met in that profession possessed, at the very least, some gray at the temple and the beginnings of permanent creases of concern on their faces. Nicholas Denman had recently crossed thirty years. He had the same stick-straight hair and beautiful blue eyes of his son, though he apparently had no need of glasses. He was perhaps five feet ten inches in height, apparently unaware he was still wearing his white physician's jacket and had very appealing masculine hands she noticed.

For his part, Nicholas was immediately less annoyed. He had expected a pinch-faced spinster, not the fashionable, olive-skinned exotic with lush piled hair and quiet searching brown eyes that stood before him. They stared silently at one another for a moment and then, remembering himself at last, Nicholas introduced himself and invited Leontine inside. He noticed that she carried the leather tool kit with her and he stiffened his resolve, understanding as he did, that she hoped to leave it behind when she left. Nicholas extended an arm directing Leontine to a chair in his sparsely furnished living room. As she seated herself, Leontine quickly took in her surroundings. The home was clean but unadorned; no pictures on the walls or pillows or rugs or ornamentation of any kind. Tesla appeared from a hallway, toenails clicking on the wood flooring. He trotted over to their guest and rested his chin briefly on her knee and allowed her one soft stroke of his head before moving a few feet away and flopping down with a sigh.

"I'm quite taken with your son, Dr. Denman," Leontine began. "I congratulate you on your abilities as a parent. Patrick told me about his mother and I am deeply sorry for you both."

"Thank you," was all Nicholas could think to say.

"I wonder if Patrick conveyed to you the lengths he went to yesterday when he came upon me fainted away in the street."

"Are you feeling ill now?"

Leontine waved the question away.

"I'm sure it was - " But she broke off realizing the topic of her corset was probably inappropriate. "Nothing."

Nicholas sighed. He could sense his resolve evaporating already and that he was hoping for guidance. She was a woman, after all, and surely any ideas she might have about child rearing would trump his own.

"I worry that Patrick did not adequately describe his kindness and helpfulness in the situation," Leontine continued, "because if he had, you would not have been able to deny my expression of gratitude."

Nicholas swiped his hand through his hair and sank onto his small mohair couch facing her. He looked out the window to De la Vina Street which was quiet at this late afternoon hour. He felt an urge to confide, squelched it and then let it rise again.

"I never know what to do. I just want him to be happy, but I don't know how to provide it. I know he hates school. I know the kids are hard on him. He's different. He's smarter than them." With some level of amusement, he admitted, "He's smarter than me."

"I can't pretend to know in a larger sense what makes a ten-year-old boy happy, but I do know he was very much drawn to this," Leontine said lifting the leather tool kit. "And I know he earned it despite his truancy."

After a moment of reflection, Nicholas said, "You're right of course, I see I should not have related the two incidents. I was gratified to hear he allowed you inside the adobe. You're the first I'm aware of."

Leontine raised an eyebrow. "It is quite something. You've been there then."

"We found it together. I had nothing to do with the transformation, however."

"And the owner of the property?" It would be difficult to bear if Patrick was somehow deprived of his fort.

"I was able to purchase the house once I realized how intensely Patrick was drawn to it, though I hope you'll keep that in confidence. The owner contacted me when a neighbor informed her Patrick was bringing things inside. I have a hard time keeping him in school. He needs the place somehow, and at least I know where he is – though I wouldn't say I know exactly what he's doing."

"The secret is safe. You are a caring father."

Leontine stood and extended the tool kit as Nicholas rose from his seat to accept it. And then suddenly there was nothing to say. Leontine immediately felt awkward and overcome by the need to escape.

"Well, thank you for understanding."

"I'll get my hat and walk with you," Dr. Denman offered.

But Leontine demurred. "I'm meeting my boarder downtown, but thank you once again."

Nicholas saw her to the door and then stood on the porch and watched her walk away from the house. Once she had turned the corner he looked at the gift for his son in one hand and swiped the other through his hair again. He never really knew what to do.

A quarter hour later, Daisy left the *Daily News*, a brick building on De la Guerra Street situated between the De la Guerra and Oreña adobes, headed out to State Street and turned right at the County Bank to meet Leontine a block up in front of Trenwith's Department Store. They peered appreciatively into the window of Lear's millinery shop next door, each expressing a desire for a new hat, marveled briefly at the oddities in the display window at Shanghai Oriental, and then sauntered down State Street in conversation, Leontine offering information and opinions about the stores, eateries and other businesses as they passed by. The two perused the menu at Delmonico's placed out on the sidewalk on a wooden tripod in front of the restaurant in an effort to entice passersby inside. They paused in front of the Mission Theater to read the lobby cards advertising a Vaudeville show coming the following month featuring *Jenny De Weese and her dog "Cuba"* to be followed by two single-reel moving pictures. On occasion Leontine would be asked to accompany the moving pictures on piano if Oliver Boyer, the usual accompanist, was otherwise occupied. She enjoyed it very much and often surprised herself with the music that would emerge from her hands as she watched the pictures unfold. Across the street stood the Lower Clock Building. The three-story Fithian Building, as it was officially named, was a most impressive Victorian structure, boasting an ornate tower that featured four Westminster clocks and chimes. As the women continued down State Street, Daisy remarked – as many had – that cigar shops, liquor wholesalers and saloons seemed to dominate the mercantile spectrum of the city.

When the women reached Stearns Wharf at the foot of State Street they marveled at the preparations already in progress for the upcoming arrival of the fleet. Stearns was a working wharf. Citizens who fancied a stroll out over the surf used the Pleasure Pier located near the Los Baños del Mar bathhouse farther west along the shoreline at the foot of Castillo Street. Dozens of banners and hundreds of garlands and thousands of flowers would soon be affixed to the wharf and along the half-mile stretch of the Boulevard to the Plaza del Mar. Looking in the direction of the Potter Hotel the women could see the grandstands already assembled in front of the bathhouse and festooned nearly to the point of obscurity, that would offer the appreciative audience a better view of the eagerly anticipated parade.

Daisy expressed her hope that the sheer magnitude of the story of the fleet might offer an opportunity to showcase her investigative prowess and skill as a journalist. So far the editor, Clarence Miller, had been dismissive of her freelance story samples. Her nature was such that his indifference only served to stoke her efforts into a blaze of determination. To her way of thinking the man had met his match in her.

The women continued west on the Boulevard enjoying the activity and energy surrounding them and made their way to the Potter where Leontine headed for the kitchens to take orders for particular groceries and supplies and Daisy to the main entry to make herself known to the desk clerks, concierge, drivers and anyone else that might have anything to say about anything whatsoever that readers might find of interest.

By the time they left the hotel the sun was low, about to sink below the far edge of the mesa bluffs. Castle Rock, a popular recreation spot, had been geologically amputated from the cliffs eons ago, and now at high tide stood ankle-deep in the surf, it's craggy shape distinctive in the diminishing light. Evenly spaced palm trees lining the ocean side of the street were becoming silhouetted in the golden slanted rays of a rose-colored sun. The trees towered some twenty feet above Ocean Boulevard, though it was said this height would seem miniscule to the altitudes they might reach in the future.

It was dusk by the time the two women made their way back toward the Birabent Market. Nevertheless, Leontine chose to walk Daisy by the old adobe, perhaps to have a peek in the window of young Patrick's fort. To their alarm and dismay they could see as they approached that the windows over the bench table had been shattered. Before Leontine could express her concern Tesla jogged up to the women and fell into step beside Leontine seeming to herd the two of them in the direction of the old house. Leontine and Daisy exchanged a look of trepidation as they approached the door. Leontine pushed it open a slight bit, calling to Patrick. Tesla, much less cautious, pushed the door fully open with his nose and hurried inside.

Patrick was nowhere in sight. Leontine's hand went to her heart as she looked around the place. Vandals had thrown large rocks through the windows and they landed on the table smashing and splintering many of the treasures thereon. At a sound from the front door the women looked up to see Patrick, dusty and disheveled, wiping grimy hands on his knee-length trousers. He seemed more calm than Leontine would have expected.

"Patrick, what happened? Are you all right? Who did this?"

Tesla moved over to his master and sat on one of his feet nudging at the boy's hand with his nose.

"I'll find out who did it," Daisy said.

"I know who," Patrick told them.

All three returned to the table to further assess the damage. Patrick seemed resigned to the maltreatment and went about quietly setting things to rights. Leontine's heart ached for the boy, seemingly more upset for him than he was for himself. Was he so accustomed to misfortune that he could no longer react? If true, it was a troubling character assessment.

"If you know who did this, Patrick, I think you should tell your father so the guilty party can be dealt with," Leontine advised.

"No! Don't say anything. He just makes it worse."

"This has happened before?" Daisy asked.

Patrick did not respond and returned his attention to cleaning up the mess. Leontine and Daisy exchanged looks of concern and then Daisy's expression transformed to one of inspiration.

"I have an idea," she told the others and even Tesla pricked up his ears to listen.

Chapter 8

Lilly White stood at the rail on the upper deck of the USS *Connecticut* marveling at the enormous crowd of people already visible who had traveled for miles to witness the fleet on its arrival in San Pedro. At some three hundred thousand souls, Los Angeles was now nearly half the size of Boston, though admittedly much larger in a geographical sense. As her eyes swept over the sea of humanity she was aware of a subtle difference from the throngs that had gathered on the east coast the preceding year. Los Angeles was a borderless expanse of burgeoning communities with increasing immigrant populations from Japan, China and the south and central Americas. Their collective energies emanated something decidedly different from the crowds dominated by those of primarily European origins on the other side of the continent.

Lilly turned to share her excitement with her aunt who was seated on a metal rectangle of some sort. Everything on this ship was covered in metal rectangles it seemed. Poor Anne had been battling seasickness since the moment they left San Diego and Lilly decided she would not attempt to coax her into sharing in the thrill of the moment. As she turned back to the view, Lilly caught movement in the corner of her eye. Just inside a cramped hallway leading to who knew where, stood Captain Adams, motioning for her to join him in the passage. Lilly glanced over her shoulder at the two sailors charged with monitoring her activities. She walked over to the young men and made intimations that she needed to step inside to do something secret of a feminine nature. Men were predictably disconcerted about the ways of women, thank goodness.

Lilly joined the Captain in the corridor, giddy with the attention and intimacy that this clandestine behavior suggested.

"Captain, I was beginning to wonder if you were even on board," she drawled, lowering her chin so she could look up at him innocently.

He said, "I don't have much time and I wonder if I could trouble you for a favor while you're in Los Angeles, Miss White."

"I'll do anything you ask, of course," she told him, as if innocently unaware of the double entendre. Adams placed a small envelope into her hand.

"This message needs to be delivered to a man named Steven Magness. I was to find him at the Westminster Hotel. It is vitally important."

What an unexpected boon for Lilly White. She had long hoped for some circumstance that would bring the two of them together, but being entrusted with a secret imperative on his behalf, well, nothing could be better suited for cementing what she saw as their budding relationship.

"Does he expect me? Will I know what to say?"

"He is expecting me. I can't say much about the circumstances, only that Rear Admiral Haines is about to make a mess of a situation he knows nothing about and he is attempting to tie my hands." Captain Adams could not disguise the disdain he felt for his commanding officer.

"He's a silly old goat and I confess it will please me to act against him. Now, tell me how I will recognize Mr. Magness."

Manipulation came easily to Lilly White, especially where men were concerned, and she found it effortless to convince her assigned detail that a detour to the Westminster was in order so that she could connect with her dear "Cousin Steven" even though the stop did not appear on their itinerary. It was helpful that their next subsequent destination was to be a rousing affair at Bullock's Department Store only a few blocks away. The Westminster was among the more fashionable hotels available in Los Angeles, though Lilly personally found the elegance wanting. As hard as it tried with Corinthian columns, coffered ceilings and giant indoor palm plants, it felt quite austere when compared with the grandeur of the hotels on the east coast. Poor Aunt Anne was so compromised from the seasickness and early hours she was only too happy to find herself in the lounge of the hotel with a glass of bitters at her elbow, whatever the atmosphere.

Lilly approached the concierge, describing Steven Magness as the Captain had described him; red hair, long sideburns and mustache. She inquired if a man fitting that description had been seen waiting anywhere nearby. He had indeed and was, even now, seated in the lobby twisting a rolled up periodical in his hands as his eyes darted to the main entry door with each new entrant. Lilly approached her detail where they had stationed themselves outside the lounge where Aunt Anne nursed her infirmities. Lilly smiled brightly, motioning to Magness seated in the lobby and explaining she would not be long in conversation with her cousin.

Magness became aware of Lilly as an obstacle to his monitoring of the main entry. Her gathered skirts obscured his immediate field of view and he leaned this way and that to see around her before finally looking into to her face with the intention of asking her to move aside. Lilly stretched out a gloved hand. Magness rose from his seat, his eyes questioning as he accepted her hand in greeting.

"Mr. Magness, I have a message for you from Captain John Adams," Lilly told him. "He sends his deepest regret that he is unable to escape the duties of the fleet." She reached into her crocheted bag and produced the written communication from the Captain. Magness' eyes narrowed with suspicion as he reached for the letter.

"I will be happy to deliver any return message for the Captain if you care to look it over now." Captain Adams had made no such request of her, but Lilly was hopeful that any response might shed light on the contents of the note. She would show John Adams that she could be trusted, an invaluable helpmate. A partner. Magness, still suspicious, opened the envelope and skimmed the few sentences scrawled on the notepaper therein.

His brow furrowed and his eyes scanned the room for a moment as he digested the contents. "Tell him I'll see him in Santa Barbara. I want a definite plan of action by then or our deal is off."

"I shall convey your statement accurately, Sir, rest assured." And she offered her hand again in parting. Magness took her hand, executed a stiff bow, and strode to the main doors in a hasty and stomping departure.

* * *

That evening, back on board the *Connecticut*, Lilly was developing a plan to steal a moment with the Captain. She had guided the conversation during dinner to learn where on the ship the Captain was expected to be after dinner and had then maneuvered circumstances so she could be planted directly in his anticipated path. Once he was spotted, Lilly asked her assigned man if he thought the Captain might be willing to grant a brief audience and expressed how grateful she would be to the crewman if he could only make that happen. She waited now as her man approached his superior officer and saw him point in her direction as he informed Captain Adams of her request. Naturally, Adams readily agreed.

Lilly delivered the response from Steven Magness, carefully assessing the reaction from Captain Adams. Strained, she thought, with a tinge of anxiety. Excellent.

She said, "I'm honored by your trust in me, Captain, and hope you might consider extending that trust in order that I might advance your enterprise, whatever it may be."

Captain Adams looked into her eyes. He saw intelligence and cunning combined with fearlessness and devotion; qualities he knew would serve all of his immediate needs. What to do with them afterward was the only thing holding him back. Lilly White was not much older than his son, a fleeting thought that made him wince for several reasons. Still, he desperately needed an ally. Rear Admiral Haines was a worthless bureaucrat but sadly, no fool. He would have had time to read the report by now and was no doubt determined to deliver the damning evidence against Allied Steel to someone higher up the chain of command or worse, to Duke White himself. The more he thought about it, the more Lilly White fitted the bill. It seemed to make sense to bring her inside the circle and he scanned his physical reaction as he considered the thought.

Captain Adams had learned in battle, on the killing fields and in the briefing rooms and offices where wars are more truly waged, that his body could provide information his thinking mind could not. It rarely disappointed when he remembered to pay attention and he searched now for a pinch in his chest or a quickening in his gut as he contemplated how deeply he might involve this enticing young woman. He felt nothing that would dissuade. Lilly watched as the thinking process played out on

Captain Adams' face, telegraphing his decision to include her in his plans before he even said the words. Lilly was, in a word, ecstatic.

As the documents were no longer in his control, Captain Adams determined his best course of action lay in neutralizing their content. If he could somehow cast suspicion on Kurt Gunn of Amalgamated Incorporated – or better yet Gunn and Rear Admiral Haines as conspirators – he could still benefit handsomely from the desperation of Steven Magness and his profitable, if morally compromised, corporation. Lilly White was more astute than he had dared hope. She grasped the varied aspects of the situation quickly and completely and he could see that their objectives were in complete alignment, the only shadowed thought being that he had been so long in finding this extraordinary feminine version of himself.

"I must arrive in Santa Barbara ahead of you," she spoke as her mind, made for scheming, began crafting the story she would influence others to play out. "Admiral Haines will be only too happy to see me on a train with poor, dear, Aunt Anne. In truth she has suffered enough."

"Maybe you can find a policeman or a businessman that would take an interest and somehow further our cause," Captain Adams suggested.

Our cause. Lilly thrilled to the sound of the phrase in her mind. "No," she countered, "a newspaperman."

And Captain Adams believed she was brilliant and beautiful and right.

Chapter 9

Patrick stood alone in the shadows at the back of the Lincoln School building. The tall windows on both floors were opened wide to circulate as much air as possible into the classrooms. The brick structure on the south-facing side of Cota near Santa Barbara Street tended to absorb warmth from the sun and hold tightly to it, thus steadily increasing the indoor temperature as the day progressed. Patrick leveled his gaze at Billy Kilgore who taunted a much younger boy with a stick, drawing it back as if to strike him. The little boy flinched. There were plenty of kids in the schoolyard, all grades having been released from their classrooms for twenty minutes to burn off fidgety energy so they could make it to the end of the school day. If any of them saw Billy terrorizing the little guy they pretended they had not. Billy snatched a small drawstring bag from the lad and was about to look inside when he seemed to sense something. He looked around to meet Patrick's stare.

"What are you looking at with those bug eyes?" Billy challenged. "Bug!" he hurled at the witness to his bullying.

"I think you threw a rock through the window of the old adobe."

"Think whatever you want," Billy said. The little boy used the distraction to make his escape. Billy glanced at the kid running away, then flicked his eyes back to Patrick as he pocketed the boy's marbles with a smirk.

"Anyways, what if I did? What're you going to do about it?" Billy goaded.

Patrick, unruffled, narrowed his eyes just a bit.

"You don't need all that junk," Billy insisted.

Silence.

"What do you need it for? Nothing, that's what," and Billy threw the stick to underscore his point.

"To summon the ghost."

"What?! You're crazy and everyone knows it, too," Billy sneered, and then he stomped around the corner of the building bumping Patrick's shoulder roughly as he went by.

Patrick smiled.

* * *

And now, the hour well past darkness, Leontine found herself perched awkwardly in the oak tree above the kitchen of the old adobe. She had initially balked at participating in this conspiracy and even now, as she heard the half dozen grade-schoolers approaching with giggles and stage whispers, she quailed at the thought of carrying the caper off knowing, as she did, what was to come next. That is until she recognized the only girl in the group. What was her name? Ah, Alice. A most unpleasant child and former piano student who failed to possess charm and talent in equal measure. And of course there was that troubled little Billy Kilgore who definitely needed a taste of his own medicine.

Leontine squirmed and tightly gripped the bulging cotton batting sheathed in black fabric that she had stitched together that very afternoon. Looking under the worktable she saw Daisy at the ready. For her part, Daisy could not have been happier. The whole affair had been her idea after all, and she was not troubled one whit by the fact that she was about to terrorize a bunch of little kids. Playing pseudo-parent to seven younger siblings had left her somewhat calloused, but she knew they would all be just fine as soon as they ran home to their mothers. This would be hilarious.

Patrick was at the head of the pack of kids and as he approached the adobe he began to tiptoe and turned to the others placing his finger against his lips motioning for them to be silent. Billy Kilgore's expression was suspicious and defiant. He didn't believe in any stupid ghost and was paying very close attention so he could expose Patrick Denman for the lying, bug-eyed baby he was. He wasn't sure why Patrick had talked the others into coming along but he was glad they were there. They would see how someone brave stands up to a ghost that probably wasn't even there because Patrick was a sneaky little liar and now everyone would know it.

Patrick crouched low and went up to the wall under the broken window. He motioned for Billy to join him and two of the other boys approached as well. Alice and the other two boys hung back. One of the little guys couldn't have been more than five years old. Patrick put his fingers on the frame below the window, and slowly lifted his head so he could peek inside. As soon as he looked inside he gasped and ducked back down quick as a flash. Billy narrowed his eyes. He wasn't buying it. The other kids weren't so sure and Alice swatted at the hand of the littlest fellow who had grabbed at her skirt in alarm. Patrick whispered loud enough for all of them to hear, but he was looking only at Billy Kilgore.

"There's light from a fire and smoke, but no fire!" he said. Then he motioned for Billy to pull himself up and look in the window to see. Billy glanced over his shoulder at the other kids and smirked, then peered in the window as Patrick had just done. His glance shot through the window into the living area and – Holy cow! – he saw it!! Billy ducked back down, his heart beating fast for a moment.

"We have to go in there," Patrick said.

Billy looked at the other kids again and nodded his head. If Patrick could do it then he could, too. They moved stealthily toward the door. Patrick eased it open and stuck his head inside. He listened for a moment as his eyes adjusted to the near-blackness, then stepped fully inside and motioned for Billy to follow. As soon as Billy got inside the door he could see a beam of light directed at the fireplace that came from the worktable.

"Hey!" He reached under a dark piece of fabric and pulled out an Ever Ready hand held cylinder light. That's what was sending the light over to the fireplace. Billy turned and was about to give Patrick a hard time about trying to scare him with such a stupid trick. The other kids were gathering at the doorway and the ones in front could already see the hoax revealed. And then, at that exact moment, Leontine tossed the dark shapeless bunting in a high arc, just as she had practiced, so that its movement would catch the peripheral vision of the kids and there would be a soft thump on the ground beside them. At the same instant,

Daisy simply reached out from beneath the table and wrapped her fingers loosely around Billy Kilgore's ankles. Billy came unhinged. He screamed like a girl and actually knocked Patrick down in his frantic escape from the room. The other kids screamed as well and ran as fast as they could after Billy. Just to make it look good Patrick followed them for a short distance but then was laughing so hard he had to fall back or be found out.

They won't be back, he thought, joyfully, and then he ran back to his friends to celebrate.

Chapter 10

The following afternoon Lilly and Aunt Anne were reclining in comfortable rocking chairs on the sun porch at the fabulous Potter Hotel. Anne, much more herself, was engaged in conversation with a not-unattractive businessman from Chicago. Those on the deck at this hour were dressed for the day's activities; tennis, bicycling, golf, swimming or simply strolling the beachfront or pleasure pier. Wait staff from the hotel glided about, balancing trays of champagne and light refreshments, as little knots of hotel guests in conversation and mellowed individuals gazed over the landscaping, the Boulevard, over the sea and out to the line of the Channel Islands beyond. Lilly tipped her head back and closed her eyes. The warmth of the sun and fresh breeze from the ocean were almost unbearably pleasant and she could hear music from somewhere. No doubt from that beautiful bathhouse she had every intention of investigating as soon as she dozed off the remaining weariness from the train trek north. She was gently stirred from her drowsiness by the soft voice of Danny Ordaz at her elbow.

"Excuse me, Miss White," he murmured. "A writer from the *Daily News* called and said she can see you whenever and wherever you like."

Upon her arrival, Lilly let it be known at the front desk that she had arrived in her capacity as hostess for the fleet and was willing to grant an interview to some lucky newspaper in advance of its arrival. She intimated there would be much more of a story than any newsman could imagine. Charlie Peavey, an energetic and earnest young doorman looking sharp in his Potter service jacket, was only too eager to deliver this exciting news to the very pretty and oh-so-interesting Daisy Merrie who had introduced herself just the day before, in hopes that she would return the favor of the information with some kindness and attention.

She. Lilly lingered on the word, never having considered she might be dealing with a female.

Danny told her, "Her name is Daisy Merrie and she's from the *Daily News*. She rents a room from my cousin and used to write for a newspaper in San Francisco. Just after the fire."

San Francisco. That was different.

"Tell her I'll see her after dinner," Lilly said, and she closed her eyes again without so much as a "thank you."

Inside in the grand lobby, Steven Magness checked into the hotel. He looked haggard, felt irritable and was hoping he could get some rest. The fleet would arrive in a day and a half and he needed his wits about him. Whatever Captain Adams was planning had better be good. Magness was ready to spend whatever it cost to turn the tides on that mealy-mouthed Puritan, Kurt Gunn. He was not aware that Kurt Gunn himself had also checked into the Potter not two hours earlier and was now napping soundly four floors above, as only those of clear conscience can do. Gunn did not know for sure what had become of the documents he entrusted to Rear Admiral Evans. Evans had promised he would deliver the scientific evidence that proved, once and for all, that Allied Steel was producing materials far inferior to the specifications approved by the Appropriations Committee of the United States congressional body.

Gunn tried several times to get the information to Senator White and was not sure at what point the evidence was repeatedly waylaid. He had been certain that the high-ranking Evans possessed a character beyond reproach and that the fraud would be exposed at last. It was suspicious that Rear Admiral Evans had taken ill. Gunn tried to see him in Paso Robles as he made his way south by train to Santa Barbara, but the staff at the sanatorium did not allow him into the Admiral's rooms. Gunn wanted to see this new man, this Haines, in person and find out if the documents had been passed along and whether or not they would be delivered to Senator White. Maybe Evans had given them to the senator's daughter. He would look for her as well.

* * *

And so it was that at seven o'clock that evening, Leontine and Daisy were seated at one of the tables in the sumptuous dining room of the Potter Hotel. Though this was far from the first time Leontine had dined at the Potter, having so recently experienced the room through the eyes of young Patrick she was more keenly aware of just how distinctive the common act of eating dinner could be. It had been easy to convince Leontine that her presence at the meeting would be advantageous and she assured Daisy she did not mind if, ultimately, she might have to disappear while Daisy got to the meat of whatever matter Miss White had in mind. Daisy did not care for the presumptuousness of the fleet hostess and vowed to assume the power position in their meeting. After all, this girl was clearly in possession of information she wanted printed. That meant Lilly White needed Daisy more than Daisy needed Lilly White. In addition, Daisy was already aware of Leontine's capacity for observation and assessment. It wouldn't hurt for Leontine to have an opportunity to direct those skills in the direction of Miss White if she were able.

In the meantime the two women enjoyed an elegant dinner and conversation.

"What do you know about a woman named Pearl Chase?" Daisy asked.

"No more than anyone, I suppose. She's at university in Berkeley and comes home for holidays. Why?"

Leontine sampled the exquisitely prepared *consommé en tassé*. She closed her eyes to enjoy the rich flavor of the impeccably clear, piping hot liquid without distraction.

"I hear she's been seen on the arm of Patrick's father," Daisy told her, and then followed suit with the *consommé*.

Leontine was a little surprised at her internal reaction. Surprised, in fact, that there had been a reaction at all. She had only seen Nicholas Denman once and remembered finding him appealing, as far as that went, but truly had not thought of him since in any capacity other than the thoughtful father of her young friend. So why did the information about Pearl Chase cause a little flutter somewhere in her chest?

"This is news at the *Daily*?"

"Civic League and Temperance Union meetings are the only assignments I've gotten outside of setting type," Daisy replied. "Their business is tame but the gossip isn't bad."

Leontine changed the subject to the matter at hand and the women considered possible motivations for the meeting requested by the worldly Miss White. They nibbled on California ripe olives, gherkins and celery served with Major Grey's Chutney until the main courses were presented; Roast Ribs of Prime Beef *au Jus* for Leontine and Potter Farm Turkey with Cranberry Jelly for Daisy. They were discussing the relative merits of walnut ice cream and sliced apple pie for dessert when Leontine became aware of the flouncing full skirts of an approaching southern belle that reason would dictate was Lilly White, and noticed her somewhat older female companion being seated one table away. Leontine was facing her approach and so was able to gain a first impression of the girl before she spoke. Body movement, Leontine had long noted, could be a far more effective display of character than conversation. Lilly White approached without looking around her. No curiosity about the renowned environment. No wondering whom else might be dining tonight. Captains of industry and political dignitaries were, after all, frequent attendees. No, this girl was on a single-minded mission and Leontine watched as she transformed her face into a winning smile as she approached the table.

"Daisy Merrie?" she said, looking back and forth between Leontine and Daisy.

Daisy rose from her seat. "Miss White." Daisy motioned in Leontine's direction. "This is my associate, Miss Birabent," she added. Lilly dipped her chin, almost like a curtsey, and then turned her attention to Daisy.

"Shall we play at being friends or will you join me at my table for some interesting information?" she asked, unmasking any pretense of pretense. Leontine saw immediately that Lilly White could have Daisy eating out of her hand. She struck the very chord that would resonate most with a journalist - direct, no nonsense and the promise of salacious detail implied. This was a woman who knew how to get what she wanted. Leontine and Daisy shared a glance that communicated Leontine should join the party. Once seated at the new table the two abandoned the contemplation of dessert and instead each requested a sherry to sip as the newer arrivals perused the menu.

If Lilly White appeared oblivious to the mouthwatering rations delivered by the gracious wait staff during the course of conversation,

Aunt Anne was engaged enough in the experience for the both of them. As Leontine quietly absorbed the tale of corporate misconduct that Miss White related to Daisy with unconstrained alarm, she smiled internally at the pleasure radiating from her Aunt Anne. Miss White, apparently sensing she was not initiating the spark of indignation she was looking for, became increasingly dramatic in her descriptions of the far-reaching and bitter consequences ahead if Kurt Gunn and his military puppet Haines were not brought to bear. Daisy did not rise to the bait, however, and in fact seemed to intentionally stoke the passions of Miss White for her own enjoyment, or perhaps to assess the limits of the young girl's acting ability. Though Lilly White was unaware, Daisy had indeed bested her in the exchange, in the end having made no promises while extracting information that would allow her to delve more deeply into the matter if she so chose.

Later, Leontine and Daisy walked up State Street heading for the *Daily News* where Daisy would work through the night. The fleet was arriving the following afternoon and it was all hands on deck for the three newspapers in town.

Daisy said, "The register from the Potter will be there by now for tomorrow's paper. If Steven Magness has checked in, I'll find him tomorrow morning."

"That is obviously what Miss White would like you to do, though I envision he will only corroborate her allegations," Leontine reasoned. "Why else point you in his direction?"

"True. She seems to be building a case, but why her – and why in the newspaper rather than a formal case tried in court? Something is odd."

"I agree."

"Miss White seems overly fond of Captain Adams. Perhaps she is his emissary - or even something more," Daisy continued. "His wife and son live in Santa Barbara. Something is wrong with the boy; retarded I think."

"How very sad," Leontine said.

"If Lilly White is his - something more, it would be cruel to be obvious about it here in Santa Barbara."

"No doubt Mrs. Adams would know little of ship building, but wives know their husbands, however estranged," Leontine maintained. "One would assume she will greet his arrival, whatever the circumstance. I can look for her while you're talking with Mr. Magness."

They approached the *Daily News* building passing in front of the De la Guerra adobe where the prominent and expansive De la Guerra family had already raised more than a generation. The courtyard of the celebrated home was strung with festive lights and lanterns and they heard the sounds of musicians tuning and playing bits of music in preparation for a night of revelry. There were many such gatherings around the city, the whole town electric with anticipation for the arrival of the fleet.

Once Daisy had disappeared into her building, Leontine turned back toward State Street and, as she walked past the sprawling adobe once more, she thought for a moment that, had Vincent not disappeared, they would no doubt be attending the gala now getting underway, Vincent being first cousins with their brood and Leontine herself related by marriage somewhere in the branches of her own family tree. For a time, before it became apparent that Vincent would, in all likelihood, not be returning, the Barón family had continued to include her in family gatherings. She was to have been one of them, after all. But as time went on Leontine began to decline their offers and shortly after that the invitations ran dry. She sighed as she passed the twinkling celebration and then returned her thoughts to more present matters

The Potter

The Dining Room

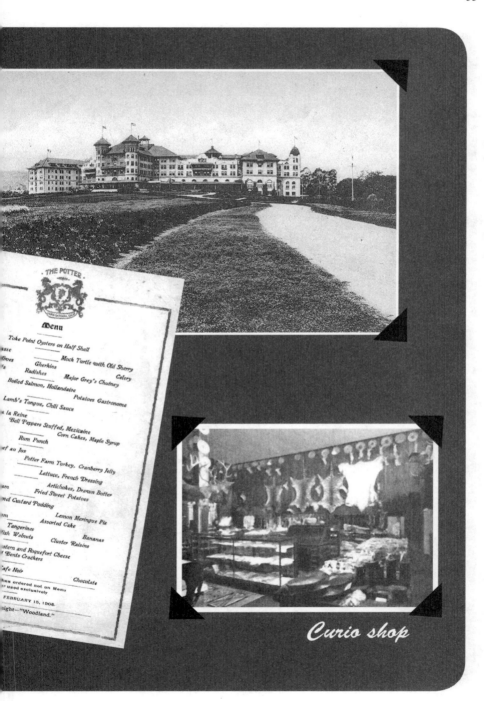

THE POTTER

Menu

Toke Point Oysters on Half Shell

asse
tives   Mock Turtle with Old Sherry
          Gherkins
's   Radishes   Celery
                    Major Grey's Chutney
Boiled Salmon, Hollandaise
                              Potatoes Gastronome
Lamb's Tongue, Chili Sauce

a la Reine
    Bell Peppers Stuffed, Mexicaine
                    Corn Cakes, Maple Syrup
      Rum Punch

ef au Jus
        Potter Farm Turkey, Cranberry Jelly
                Lettuce, French Dressing
                Artichokes, Drawn Butter
am   Fried Sweet Potatoes
nel Custard Pudding
                    Lemon Meringue Pie
m   Assorted Cake
  Tangerines
lish Walnuts   Bananas
                Cluster Raisins
stern and Roquefort Cheese
 Bents Crackers

afe Noir
                                Chocolate
hen ordered not on Menu
r used exclusively

FEBRUARY 15, 1908.

night—"Woodland."

Curio shop

56

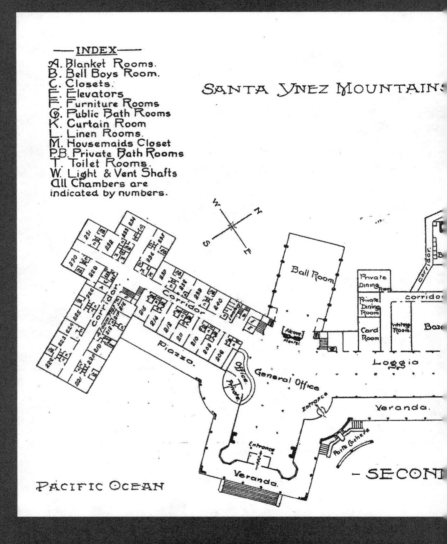

SANTA YNEZ MOUNTAINS

Ball Room

Private Dining Room

Private Dining Room

corridor

Card Room

Writing Room

Box

Corridor

Loggia

Corridor

Corridor

Piazza

Office Private

General Office

Entrance

Veranda.

Porte Cochere

Entrance

Veranda.

PACIFIC OCEAN

– SECOND

Potter Hotel Sail Boats, Santa Barbara, Cal.

West wing 5th floor Potter Hotel

Ensign
Stroud

Captain
Adams

Rear Admiral
Haines

Rear Admiral Haines' suite

Entrance to the Potter Hotel from S. P. Depot,
Santa Barbara, Cal.

*Chapala Street entrance
to Potter Hotel from train station*

Sailors Parade at the Flower Festival, Santa Barbara, Calif., April 28, 1908.

"The Battle of the Flowers"

State St., Santa Barbara, Cal.

State Street 900 block looking towards ocean

Snow on the mountains!

Customer, Papa, Mama, me & Uncle Remi

A view inside our market

Chapter II

Captain John Adams was not accustomed to losing sleep. He was often well rested in circumstances that left other men haunted and exhausted and his ability to rest in difficult situations was one of the ways he maintained his store of energetic magnetism. Not so tonight. In the darkest hour he came close to a change of heart. He was relatively young after all, and surely there would be other opportunities for financial gain. He would find a champion or another scheme. There had to be an easier way. Rear Admiral Haines was a stone wall, Magness a hothead, and Gunn a self-righteous do-gooder. It was impossible to reason why Rear Admiral Evans had brought him into this web of intrigue. Was he trying to help somehow or only protecting himself? There was just no way to know.

Lilly was a more than able accomplice, but what on earth was he to do about his wife and son? For the last decade he had spent little time with his family. He loved Elizabeth once. She was bright and lively and filled with pride in her husband's accomplishments. That was before Quincy. John Quincy Adams was his full name, actually. By the time they understood the depth of his handicap they had already bestowed the dynastic moniker. Now it seemed an embarrassing joke. Adams had been unable to reconcile with the turn of events and knew in his heart that he had, for all intents and purposes, abandoned his fragile family like a coward. He knew it, but was not shamed by the knowledge, which might indeed indicate he would be able to stomach the daily horror of abhorrent decisions one must face in the Oval Office.

It made no sense to blame his wife, and yet somehow that is what he did. Elizabeth well knew his aspirations, and knew also he would never gain his prize if he abandoned the tragedy of his son in actuality and so she made herself content as the remote yet outwardly devoted wife of really nothing more than a career. Captain Adams imagined the two of them awaiting his arrival and what his men would think and say when they got a look at his son. He felt trapped, desperate and humiliated, and above all, resentful for having to think about it at all. Finally he gave up his bunk, dressed and went on deck for a smoke. The other ships were invisible, the waning moon having moved on for the night. He acknowledged the hands on deck and then leaned against the railing to watch the turmoil of the sea far below in the running lights of the ship. He had explained to Elizabeth in a letter that he was not on leave and would be staying at the Potter Hotel with the other senior officers during their stay in Santa Barbara and in all likelihood would be unable to spend any time with her at all. She had not sent a response – nor did he expect one. She always behaved as instructed.

He hoped that Lilly had found her mark and began to sequence in his mind the steps it would take to tarnish the polished reputation of the Bureaucrat Haines and the Squealer, Kurt Gunn. Not so difficult, really. Now, in this moment he could not even remember why he had considered throwing in the towel not half an hour earlier.

It was just before sunrise and Captain Adams was about to return to his cabin when he was summoned to the Rear Admiral's office. If it was Haines' intention to keep him aboard ship while in Santa Barbara he was sunk. He was prepared to make a case for going ashore and was not above using his unfortunate son as a reason. He acknowledged the Ensign manning the desk outside the Rear Admiral's door, stepped inside the office and snapped a salute. He tried his best to ignore the limp-wristed response.

"Sir," Captain Adams barked.

"As ranking officer I will deliver the speeches at scheduled events. You are relieved of that duty."

"Yes, Sir."

"Dismissed,.

Adams spun out of the room. Was he kidding? Captain Adams was a stirring speaker and, though he had been looking forward to some pseudo-stumping in front of a large crowd, it was far down the list of critical matters on his mind. Poor crowd. Just a few minutes of Haines' nasal high-pitched droning could put a mosquito to sleep. He bounded up the ladder leading to the top deck and took his place to begin the orchestration of a dazzling display that would thrill and astonish the citizens in the peaceful little town of Santa Barbara.

Back in his office, Rear Admiral Haines still held the telegram he had received from his brother half an hour before Captain Adams reported to his office. Percifal's father had died at the veteran's retirement facility a week ago. His brothers originally thought to wait until he had completed his mission and docked in San Francisco to tell him of the passing, but later considered Haines might want to know before the old man was interred. A week. Funny how the Rear Admiral had just been considering how best to wrest the psychological command from Captain Adams that had eluded him thus far; to transfer the unseen mantle of power to himself, and had actually wondered what the old man might do in his place. Or even his brothers, as much as he normally disagreed with their tactics - not that he would have seriously considered seeking their actual counsel. Still, it seemed fitting somehow. He looked inside to see if he felt sorrow. No. None. Relief? Not that either. He looked and looked but in truth he felt nothing at all.

He should have felt anger at the very least, he reasoned. After all, his brothers kept the information from him for an entire week. That he had not communicated with any of them for years was not an excuse. They knew where to find him. They delivered the message he held now in his hand, did they not? He was more resolute than ever to raise himself up in the eyes of the crew. The more men were made to look up to you literally the more they were inclined to do so figuratively, he told himself, which was his reasoning behind delivering the speeches at the parade and other festive gatherings. He would supplant the strutting Captain as the anointed leader. His father would no doubt have approved, though if he did, it would have been the first time. The old man had only been gone for a week and already Percifal seemed to have reaped some psychic benefit.

Still, he thought, *a week...*

Chapter 12

Later that morning Leontine and Daisy walked down State Street toward Stearns Wharf, taking the long way to the Potter so they could marvel at the last of the preparations for the arrival of the fleet. They had dressed for the occasion, as had nearly everyone in town. Leontine looked appropriately elegant for the daytime event in her charmeuse day dress in palest apricot with intricately embroidered appointments at the bodice and hemline in white silk thread. Her broad brimmed hat in the same delicate shade was decorated with hand crafted white satin roses as was the trim of the white lace parasol, and the entire ensemble caused her creamy caramel-colored skin and golden brown eyes to appear all the more exotic. Though Daisy was slightly shorter and just a whisper thicker in the waist, Leontine found something suitable in her wardrobe for her boarder to borrow as well. The white linen summer dress had a full skirt with sky blue ribbon at the waist and hat brim. There was a matching parasol for this outfit as well but Daisy left it behind, deciding against the bother carrying it.

The arrival was anticipated for mid-afternoon and Barbareños were heading for every possible vantage point, dragging along food and drink to make an entire day of it. As the women rounded the corner at the Boulevard they were swept into a current of humanity, one-quarter of the town's residents flowing toward the sound of the City Orchestra already stoking the festive atmosphere in front of the Plaza del Mar bathhouse.

Daisy was eager to find Steven Magness, who, she learned, had indeed checked into the Potter the day before. Not only that, she had seen the name of Kurt Gunn as well. Was Lilly White aware? Was Magness? There seemed opportunity in this knowledge but Daisy couldn't quite get a grasp of how best to use it. She decided to trust her instincts and split off from Leontine to make a more determined approach to the hotel with a promise to connect later.

Leontine said, "Locating Mrs. Adams in this crush may prove impossible."

"I'd look for the son," Daisy advised, as she hurried away.

As Leontine made her way west on the Boulevard she saw families with young children, older children running in packs, strolling couples and enthusiastic elders, all shuffling between a myriad of street vendors and delighting in presentations from jugglers and magicians, preachers and spiritualists and even an artist who would sketch your likeness on fine vellum for twenty cents. Her senses filled with the sights and smells from dozens of food carts intertwined with the salty musk from the sea and the scents and sounds of a thousand people. Local artisans had invented endless ways to hitch their wares to a naval theme. There were cards with images of the mighty vessels of the fleet and information about each one printed on the reverse side. Buttons and election-type badges were lined up on tabletops showing likenesses of President Roosevelt, Secretary of War, William Howard Taft, and many of the more decorated officers in the fleet. Food vendors stayed on topic as best they could, at the very least poking miniatures of Old Glory into the tops of their meat pies, beverages and confections.

Leontine became aware of a couple strolling in her direction, then finally recognized Nicholas Denman and, on his arm, the stylish and confident Pearl Chase. Pearl was a practical woman and purchased her ready-made clothing from the several boutique shops or even Collins-Walton Department Store next to Brown's piano store just above Ortega Street. Nevertheless, she looked quite smart in a blush-colored day suit with wide satin lapels in a complimentary rose color, a high collared lace blouse beneath and a delicate satin bowtie at the neck in the rose satin. Her broad brimmed chocolate-brown felt hat sported an exceedingly lush white plume that wrapped around the hat brim and curved toward her cheek in quite an alluring manner. The University at Berkeley apparently offered plenty of down time for their over-achieving scholars Leontine thought uncharitably to herself and then internally shook her head at the unkind thought and acknowledged that of course, this week was special.

Leontine did not see Patrick at first. He tagged along sullenly several paces behind his father with his chatting consort. Once in sight, Leontine kept her eyes on the young boy. He had not seen her yet, but when he did she would get him to smile. At the sight of Leontine, Patrick's face lit up and he brushed past his father and Miss Chase and immediately ran to his friend. Leontine knelt down to receive him eye to eye and they greeted with a quick hug. Leontine brushed the hair from his eyes with affection as she rose to address the approaching couple. Pearl was the first to speak.

"Good afternoon, Leontine. Nicky, you've never told me Patrick is learning piano," she pretended to scold. "How lovely."

Leontine shot a glance at Patrick's father to see if he would be the one to correct the mistaken observation, but it was Patrick who piped up.

"She's not my teacher," he said. Leontine rested a hand lightly on Patrick's shoulder.

"Patrick and I have become friends."

Miss Chase could not stop one eyebrow from rising as she registered the information. Her eyes narrowed for just a moment and she looked Leontine up and down, attempting to assess any level of competition.

"We have several interests in common," Leontine continued. "Dr. Denman, how nice to see you again."

Nicholas tipped his bowler hat, and though he spoke to Leontine, she could not help wondering if his comment was more directed to Miss Chase. "Please call me Nicholas."

Leontine knelt once more to speak quietly to Patrick. "I'm trying to find the family of the Captain of one of the ships. Do you want to come with me?"

Patrick lifted his arm as he responded and Leontine grasped his hand before he could wipe his nose. He wiggled his upper lip back and forth in an attempt to stop his nose itching without the use of his hand.

"Dad, may I please I go with Miss Birabent?"

Nicholas and Patrick locked eyes, communication apparently flowing between them. Pearl was obviously delighted with the suggestion. All three looked to the physician with a single desire: his assent.

"I'll be watching the arrival on the veranda of the Potter Hotel. If you make your way there this afternoon I'll do my best to gain access for you. At the worst I can return your son to you in the lobby."

Patrick's face adopted a pleading look. *Ah, poor Dr. Denman,* Leontine thought. She saw the look in his eye, wanting to share the excitement of the day with his son and yet needing to divide his attention with an admittedly worthy and attractive young woman. She sensed he was filling neither role to his own satisfaction. He reached down and ruffled Patrick's hair.

"If that's what you want to do," he agreed, and Patrick squinched up his face in that adorable smile.

"Two o'clock in the lobby."

"We'll see you there," Nicholas said.

Leontine nodded slightly in the direction of Miss Chase.

"Pearl."

And Miss Chase dipped her chin in return.

"Leontine."

Patrick, still holding Leontine's hand, allowed himself one skipping step and then matched her pace. The day was suddenly looking up. Leontine had decided on full disclosure where Patrick was concerned. She purchased a doughy, fried and sugary confection from a Mexican street vendor and sat on a bench with her young companion enjoying the treat and the crowd of people swarming around them.

"I want to talk to the Captain's wife about something the fleet hostess told Daisy last night," Leontine explained. "She said there are some business people who are committing a crime and that the head of the whole fleet is involved. She made it seem she is acting on behalf of a Captain of one of the ships who wants to reveal the wrong-doing of his commander."

Patrick thought it over as he took another bite of sticky sweetness. "What would the Captain's wife know? She's not even in the navy."

"That's true, of course, but nearly anyone can be presented in a bad light - or a good one for that matter. We need to learn who is more likely to behave badly."

Patrick nodded. He could see that.

"Do you know the Captain's son? His name is Quincy."

Patrick gave an exaggerated nod as he chewed the last bite of his treat.

"He's pretty old but they were going to put him in my grade. He only came one day though. I never talked to him, but I saw him. He's…." Patrick couldn't think how to describe him.

"I know," Leontine said, to relieve him of trying. The two of them sauntered all the way down to the Plaza to catch a glimpse of the City Orchestra before doubling back on the other side of the street and heading up the grounds to the Potter. Broad walkways wandered through flowerbeds overflowing with Easter lilies, freesia, ranunculus and mums – among many others. The grounds had been manicured and spotless at early morning, but the swarm of visitors was already taking a toll. Jacketed staff members in continuous motion gave directions, looked for missing friends or answered inquiries of varied nature to the best of their abilities as the well-heeled, connected or simply fortunate gathered at the grand hotel with its unobstructed view of the channel. Patrick pointed to the sixth-floor sunroof that already held so many people it was concerning. There appeared to be a face in every window and an uninterrupted flow of people coming and going and going and coming through front and side entrances alike.

* * *

Meanwhile, Daisy had found her man in the gentlemen's lounge on the first floor down a short hallway situated between the game room and the Curio Shop. The place was filled to capacity with more than fifty men and, because of the imminent event, a few women as well. Typically that would not be the case at this relatively early hour, though the fact would not have dissuaded Daisy from entering. She had fished her own father out of many a drinking establishment and often found herself quite liking the typical barroom atmosphere. The few weeks she spent tagging along with Eddie Franks, an apprentice writer at the *San Francisco Chronicle*, had found her in more drinking establishments than even her old man and his mates at the docks. In truth, those weeks with Eddie amounted to the sum total of her experience in journalism and though affections had cooled for the boy fairly quickly she would be forever grateful to him for the introduction to what was clearly a life's passion. This Potter lounge was far from the average bar however, so Daisy was relieved at the presence of the other women and of her stylish dress so kindly supplied by Leontine.

Magness had not slept as well as he had hoped. His nerves were raw and the noise and activity around him grating. Lilly White had found him in this same bar the evening before and laid out the plan conceived by Captain Adams; to preempt the release of the damning evidence with allegations of lies and trickery, and told him to expect a visit from a woman from the local newspaper, now seated across from him. Daisy joined him in a morning jolt – whiskey, though it was barely noon. She raised her glass in a mock toast, then downed the elixir in one go and set the empty glass gently on the table. She was no shrinking violet; he'd give her that.

She said, "I don't think the readers of the *Daily News* would take much to hearing that the admiral of the fleet is a villain. Not right now."

"Obviously. What else does Gunn need him for? People are stupid. They'll believe anything if it comes from the military."

"There are laws against libel."

Magness snorted in disgust. "By the time any trial got started I'd be sunk. The only way to protect myself is to strike first." He polished off his whiskey, then lifted his hand to the bartender to order another. He glanced at Daisy who nodded that she would join him. He caught the bartender's eye and showed him two fingers, then scowled at the deafening noise of the crowd around them.

Daisy asked, "What's in it for Lilly White?"

"Nothing. I don't know. She's sweet on the Captain."

"What's in it for him?"

"I won't lie. I offered him money to help me out. I needed to even the odds, you know?"

"My experience is that people say 'I won't lie' just before they start lying."

"Why would I lie about something that makes me look bad?"

"Adams looks worse."

The whiskey arrived and the two sat in silence for a moment.

"You know he's here, right?" Daisy said. "Kurt Gunn? He arrived just ahead of you."

Magness threw the liquor down his throat, breathed through the burn and glared around him.

"I'm not surprised," he admitted, and then he looked Daisy straight in the eyes, unflinching, like liars do, and asked, "Will you help me?"

Daisy watched his face, mostly wanting to see how long he could hold onto the expression of innocence. Longer than she cared to wait, it turned out. She stood and pushed her drink closer to the businessman deciding he could use it more than she.

"We'll see," she replied cryptically, and left him scowling in the bar as she headed for the lobby, wondering how on earth she would find Kurt Gunn in this swarm of people. It took a while to make her way to the front desk. She knew before she posed the question to the overwhelmed desk clerk that it was doubtful he would be able to help her.

"I'm hoping to locate one of your guests: Kurt Gunn. I wonder if you know where I might find him." She had to grin at the ridiculousness of the request. The desk clerk was grateful for that grin and as a result was more willing to help her.

"Would you like to leave a message for him?"

"He wouldn't know to look for it. Could you deliver a message to his room?"

"Yes, but it might take some time."

She saw no other recourse and stood by while he retrieved some hotel stationery and a fountain pen.

Daisy moved to a bench near the wall and perched on the edge of the seat as she tapped the pen against her teeth and deliberated on the content of the note. How to entice without putting Gunn on guard was the task. Difficult, given she had no clue as to his character. Or did she? He was the one motivated to bring in outside influence after all, presumably to correct what he perceived as sinister and underhanded actions. She put pen to paper:

Dear Mr. Gunn,
I have been made aware of circumstances of paramount
importance to you. Others have solicited my assistance,
however, conscience dictates that I reach out to you
before taking any action. Please leave a message with the
front desk if you would grant an audience.
*   Daisy Merrie,*
*   The Daily News*

She read it through a few times and could not think how to improve it and so, smiling, delivered it into the hand of the desk clerk. Her next self-imposed task was to find the optimum location from which to view the arrival of the fleet. The writing staff at the *Daily* would, of course, cover the event, but it was her intention to submit an account that might surpass all their collective efforts. To her unending delight she spotted Charlie Peavey patiently attempting to respond to the needs of some wealthy matrons hoping to somehow reserve territory in the sun parlor in order to best view the arrival, yet having no desire to save the space with their actual physical presence. Charlie was only too happy to turn his attention to Daisy and offered to deliver her personally to the sixth-floor roof garden, a location reserved only for the exceedingly privileged. She followed him willingly and thought briefly of Leontine, but decided her preferential treatment was more likely to continue if she proceeded on her own. As they waited in front of the elevator Daisy stared steadfastly at the sliding doors, as did Charlie. She felt a twinge of guilt knowing that the young man's shyness would keep him helpful, yet forever at arms length if she allowed it to unfold that way.

* * *

Leontine held tight to Patrick's hand worried that she would lose track of him in the crowd. She was growing weary of the crush of people and felt torn between finding a quiet corner of respite and continuing her search for the elusive Mrs. Adams. They walked the entire width of the hotel from side to side, inside and out and now her feet were tired and sore. Her white leather slippers with scalloped closure and eight side buttons were relatively comfortable as they were well worn, but no footwear would be up to a task so protracted. She suggested to Patrick that they attempt to find a place to sit for a moment on one of the benches situated in the many gardens. No sooner had she sunk gratefully onto the wooden seat, than she felt Patrick nudge her arm. He pointed toward another walkway that skirted the outside perimeter of the grounds and led directly out to the Boulevard. There she saw a woman who was unmistakably the object of their search as evidenced by the moon-faced, plodding teen at her side. The boy was slightly taller than his mother and no small amount heavier. Leontine and Patrick put their heads together quickly to arrive at a plan of action. They then hurried to an alternate pathway that would intersect with the one traveled by the mother and son near the main walk along the Boulevard. When Mrs. Adams and her son drew near, they found Leontine seated on a bench watching Patrick as, on hands and knees in the garden, he swiped at green foliage beneath the robust blossoms of a healthy stand of agapanthus, apparently looking for something. Patrick stood as the two approached and waved at the other boy.

"Hey Quincy," he called out, "Remember me from school? I'm looking for my ship's whistle. It fell in the plants."

He turned back to his task. Mrs. Adams' face registered surprise and then a measure of cautious delight that someone had spoken to her son. Quincy, aware that something had lightened the mood of his mother, though oblivious to the cause, smiled at her, ignoring Patrick completely. Leontine rose from her seat and addressed the Captain's wife.

"Are you escaping the madness? I confess I may change my mind as well."

Patrick directed another comment to young Quincy. "Want to help me look? I'll let you give it a try if you find it first."

Quincy had no real idea what was being asked of him, but he was happy at the attention and smiled broadly at everyone. His open and friendly demeanor touched Leontine.

"Come on," Patrick coaxed and made exaggerated motions of searching in the bushes to try to show Quincy what he meant. Quincy let go of his mother's hand and plodded over to Patrick, then laughing, stepped off the walkway and began stomping in the landscaping. Leontine winced internally, sending a silent apology to the gardening staff at the hotel. She left Patrick to occupy the boy and turned her attention to the mother.

"I should have realized most of the town would hope for a spot at the Potter," she lamented. She eyed Mrs. Adams more carefully and saw the lines of stress and weariness around her eyes and the grim line of her mouth.

"Yes, it is overwhelming."

Her eyes darted continually to her son. She was not accustomed to kind attention from other children and stood ready to intervene at the least sign of agitation.

"Patrick said he met your son at Lincoln School one day."

Elizabeth Adams pursed her already pursed lips, the memory apparently an unpleasant one.

"Your son is very kind. Most of the children were not, I'm sorry to say."

Leontine decided in the moment to let stand the mistaken observation that Patrick was her son.

"Is he excited by the ships?" Leontine asked, changing the subject. She was trying only to extend the conversation, carefully feeling her way along. Mrs. Adams looked at Quincy who was now rolling around in the dirt. She knew she should probably make him stop but fourteen years had taught her to pick her battles. She let him roll.

"His father is Captain of the *Connecticut*," she said. "But he doesn't even really know what a ship is."

Leontine could think of no response and shifted her gaze to the boys.

"I'm afraid it's all too taxing. I hope you enjoy the day," the mother said, and then went to encourage her gigantic child to stand so she could get him home. Patrick assisted her efforts by making a game of jumping up. Quincy got the idea and moments later Patrick and Leontine watched the pair continue away, somehow a part of the beachfront crowd and yet distinctly separate from everyone else. Patrick looked up to Leontine, his magnified blue eyes clouded with compassion. She ruffled his hair, heaved a big sigh and attempted to lighten his heart.

"Let's go find Cousin Danny and see if he can get us a place for the show. Then we'll try to find your father."

One of the benefits of youth is the ability to switch gears nearly instantaneously and Leontine was relieved to see Patrick's expression change quickly to one of eager anticipation. She turned for another look at Elizabeth Adams. She saw a woman alone shouldering unbearable hardship and knew without doubt that the husband she had not yet met was behaving badly. It diminished her own anticipation and left her feeling suspicious of the motives of young Lilly White. She wondered how Daisy was faring with Steven Magness.

* * *

An hour later Leontine and Patrick were stationed at the railing on the coveted veranda. Rocking chairs and side tables had been cleared so that more spectators could be packed into the space. Danny promised to deliver Dr. Denman and Miss Chase to their location so they would not risk losing their spot in searching for them and he affixed a Teddy Roosevelt button to Patrick's collar and provided the boy with two small replicas of the American flag with its forty-five stars – lack of time precluding the inclusion of the new state of Oklahoma's forty-sixth - and thirteen stripes; one to wave in each hand. When Nicholas and Miss Chase arrived it was apparent, and somewhat awkward, that Patrick intended to remain at Leontine's side. She did her best to keep the boy situated close to his father so they could share the moment of the arrival and received a look of gratitude from the father for her effort. It made Leontine smile and she felt something like a blush creeping up her neck and so turned her gaze toward the sea and away from the good doctor and his companion. A quarter of an hour passed in somewhat stilted conversation, and then the attention of all became riveted on the sea to the south. So that he could see over the adults around him, Patrick accepted his father's offer to pick him up, though he would never have allowed such childish treatment in any other situation. Nicholas strained a bit under the weight of his boy but was clearly deeply pleased. Pearl and Leontine were destined it seemed to experience the exciting moment together. Both women kept their eyes focused seaward.

It was approximately three p.m. when the first of the sixteen battleships appeared at the far end of the channel. For some time the fleet steamed westward as though Santa Barbara were to be passed by a wide margin. Then, to the astonishment of all who had never seen a fleet maneuver, the ships turned as one and headed straight for the city. Perhaps half way in, they turned in unison and again steered westward along the channel. Then, at just the right moment, they turned a third time and, in complete silence came straight toward the Boulevard. There was not a sound. Slowly the ships seemed to grow larger and larger as they "drifted" nearer and nearer to the shore. An unseen signal was given and the anchor chains on each ship rattled as the fleet reached its berth. It was an amazing spectacle. As the anchors dropped into the water, the crowd on the beach went wild. There was a roar of welcome that was deafening and the entire city immediately gave itself over to merrymaking.

As the crowd on the veranda began to disperse, Leontine knelt and whispered something softly in Patrick's ear. His face lit up and he looked over to his dad.

"Can I show you something?" the boy asked his father with a tempting grin. Nicholas smiled in return and took his son's hand. As they walked away without even a glance at the two women, Leontine and Pearl could hear Patrick explaining cheerfully about the Brunswick bowling lanes, the animal heads in the Curio Shop and the separate room made just for ping-pong.

The temporarily abandoned women exchanged somewhat tight-lipped smiles and then both turned their eyes away, one to gaze idly at the surrounding sea of humanity, one to the shoreline and the massive fleet of ships now silhouetted in the slanted rays of the late afternoon sun. It was Pearl who broke the silence.

"I suppose you will attend the formal event in the ballroom on Monday evening. It promises to be quite an affair," she ventured.

"No, I'll miss it I'm afraid."

Pearl's look turned inward for a moment as she thought something over. When she arrived at a decision, she took a breath and leveled her gaze at Leontine with an air of someone about to confide.

"Nicholas has been invited to the ball and I feel certain he would attend but for needing to care for Patrick."

Naturally Leontine understood immediately what was on Pearl's mind but for some reason decided to force her to articulate her desire.

"He is an attentive father."

"Leontine, I wonder if you would be a dear and invite Patrick to spend that evening with you. The two of you are obviously close and I dare to hope that Nicky might invite me to join him if he knew his son was happy and well cared for. I'm returning to Berkeley the next morning and won't have another chance to celebrate."

In truth Leontine loved the idea. Danny had easily procured an invitation for her but she had not yet made the decision to use it in any case.

"I'll do that, yes."

Pearl was relieved and delighted. "You are a dear. I can't tell you how much I appreciate this. We women must stick together."

Leontine quite liked the feeling that Pearl Chase owed her one. It could well come in handy one day.

Chapter I3

The following morning, Sunday, found Leontine and Patrick among the throngs of people moving in excited clusters around the city of Santa Barbara, Tesla close at their heels, his head and tail held high as if infused by the collective energies of the humans around him. Leontine had learned her lesson the previous day and was sure to wear her most comfortable walking shoes that in any case went quite well with her navy gored skirt and white cotton blouse with lace appliqués. She and Patrick had agreed to skip the services planned at the Old Mission for the townspeople and four hundred crewmen, twenty-five having been invited from each ship. Instead, they began their entertainments with the band concert at City Park between Micheltorena and Sola Streets. Dr. Denman had promised to attend the Mission service with Miss Chase and so would join them at the first of two scheduled baseball games at the athletic field near the Plaza del Mar on Castillo Street.

While attending the concert Leontine was interested to get a look at Captain Adams and Rear Admiral Haines who were introduced from the bandstand, along with Miss Lilly White, where they observed from a roped-off section of chairs situated for the comfort of important representatives of the fleet. Lilly White rarely removed her gaze from the Captain and her infatuation was so apparent that Leontine found herself looking around for his wife and son, thinking to distract them from seeing the same thing should they be in attendance. She saw the officers and the hostess again not two hours later as the first baseball game was getting underway. Rear Admiral Haines spoke unintelligibly into a microphone that caused static-y speakers to screech in shrill protest as some poor unfortunate tried to boost the thing high enough to pick up his faint voice. Lilly White did somewhat better and certainly kept the attention of the young men surrounding her whether or not they could understand her enthusiastic introduction of the ball game.

When Dr. Denman found Patrick and Leontine, without Miss Chase it had to be noted, the two were in the stands cheering the local team as it trotted onto the baseball diamond. None of the three could suppress broad smiles as the fun and excitement of the gathered crowd washed over them. Nevertheless, Leontine excused herself after a very short time. Though the Birabent Market was normally closed on Sunday, she and Uncle Remi had agreed that the dramatically increased activity downtown would no doubt yield extra money in the coffers. It was her intention to relieve her uncle of the extra duty however, as he had done far more than his share since the arrival of the fleet. It filled her heart also to think of Patrick basking in his father's undivided attention. She felt quite certain the two had not shared enough lighthearted moments together and she vowed to do all she could to assist any such ventures if she were able.

That evening, worn out from what had proved to be a busier afternoon in the market than even she and Uncle Remi had anticipated, Leontine and Daisy shared a light supper of cold chicken and potato salad that would not last another day in the ice box. They took their repast into the living room so they could gaze over State Street as they ate and chatted about the day's events and those upcoming. Naturally talk turned to Lilly White, Captain Adams and the brewing corporate scandal.

"I found an article written by Kurt Gunn for the *San Francisco Chronicle*," Daisy said. "It had a photograph, but not a very good one. It is fairly recent though, and definitely better than nothing. At least I have an idea of who I'm looking for."

"What will you say to him if you find him?"

"The article laid out his side of the story; that Allied Steel should not provide materials for government contracts and that his company would be a better choice, but I'd like to know why he thinks Lilly White and the United States Navy seem so set against him."

"One does wonder at motives all around," Leontine agreed.

Daisy's eyes tracked back and forth as she fell into thought for a moment, then she pursed her lips and spoke somewhat dispiritedly.

"None of this has anything to do with anyone in Santa Barbara. Clarence Miller probably wouldn't print anything I would write about it in any case. He didn't include the *Chronicle* article in the *Daily* when he had the chance. Still, it's something to try."

"No doubt even our interest will fade once the ships sail, though I confess I feel quite caught up by it at the moment. I feel concern for Mrs. Adams," Leontine admitted. "I believe I'll seek her out with an offer of tea and company. Patrick seems willing to entertain Quincy and I'm sure even a brief respite from the solitary care of her son would be welcome."

The night now in full darkness, their gazes settled on the window, which only reflected back their quiet conversation in the cozy room. They lingered a bit longer, listening through the silence to the noises in the street below and then the two finally trudged off to bed.

* * *

The following day Patrick and his father turned up at the market at early afternoon. Patrick breathlessly described for Leontine the daylight fireworks display they had just witnessed at the beach put on by the local Japanese community. The next big event was the grand floral parade that would begin in another hour and Patrick was hoping she could get away to see it with him. Though local children had been let out of school for the entire week, adults still had to earn a living and so Nicholas was returning to his office in the Eddy Building. The parade was to end with a "Battle of the Flowers" at the reviewing stand in front of the Plaza del Mar followed by more music and undoubtedly more speeches. Uncle Remi was content to stay at the store, admitting frankly that he had little interest in battling flowers, crowds or anything else. Leontine disappeared to quickly change into a starched white cotton shirtwaist with navy pinstriped skirt and broad-brimmed sun hat as the day was exceedingly warm. Daisy was at work, but Uncle Remi assured them he would point her in their direction if she turned up.

Leontine and Patrick squeezed themselves into the crowded stands lining the Boulevard between Stearns Wharf and the Plaza del Mar for a choice view of the floral procession as it passed between the ranks of sailors on one side of the street and the closely packed tribune seats of the spectators on the other. Once the fifteen hundred marching crewmen reached the Plaza, they circled before the reviewing stand of Rear

Admiral Haines and his officers and then countermarched to the foot of the Boulevard, greeted at every step by cheers, as it then turned again to repeat the march. The "turning" was the signal for the battle to begin. From every hand came a shower of flowers, bright blossoms of brilliant yellow, deepest purple and purest white, until they formed a plush fragrant carpet as soft as velvet. Back and forth they pelted each other, the people in the stands and the horsemen and occupants of floats, carriages and autos. It was a "battle" that ended in triumph for all.

Time was spent wandering the Boulevard and enjoying lively music and dancing at the Plaza, and so it was some hours later that Leontine and Patrick returned to the apartment spent and famished from the day's activity. They had gathered up Tesla from the old adobe on the way there where he had been napping, apparently as weary of the hordes as Uncle Remi, and he now made himself comfortable on an old horse blanket on the kitchen floor Leontine had laid out for just that purpose. She scared up some milk, fresh bread, butter and honey and left Patrick on his own with the snack while she went into her room to remove her hat and freshen up. She returned to find him looking at the photograph on the mantle, having set it upright.

The picture showed Leontine at roughly Patrick's age sitting astride a horse along with her mother and father, also mounted, posing for a photographer before they went off for a day of riding and picnicking in Mission Canyon.

"It fell over," Patrick explained with a hint of sheepishness.

"Did it," Leontine replied, more statement than question.

Of course, he knew she was on to him, and that he meant only to satisfy his own curiosity and would no doubt have returned the photo to its face as he found it had Leontine not entered the room.

"Why don't you want to see it?"

"It makes me feel sad," Leontine admitted. "I leave it there because I hope one day I might be able to look at it and feel happy instead."

Patrick moved along the mantle and replied in the off-hand way children have of speaking truth. "It seems more sad because it's lying down."

Leontine looked at the image of her young self in the photograph and remembered how impossibly close the islands had seemed that day and how she had seen her mother blush and smile at some secret comment spoken quietly by her father. She realized then that Patrick was right and left the picture as he had placed it.

He then picked up the brass bell and read its inscription:

"For Lulubelle"

He turned a questioning look to Leontine.

"It was my father's nickname for me," she said, with a slight smile. Patrick then moved over to her Shiedmayer Model 20 grand piano and lifted the lid covering the ivory keys as he simultaneously asked permission to do so with his eyebrows. Leontine slid in beside him on the bench and entertained him with a rollicking thirty seconds of music, then showed him a few things so he could make a pleasing sound. He had an ear she was gratified to learn.

While they were at it Daisy blew in, a bundle of frustration-fueled energy. She bemoaned the time lost in the toil of typesetting and worried that she would be unable to pick up any threads in the little time remaining before everyone she was interested in disappeared out of reach into the grand ballroom of the Potter Hotel. She had no invitation for the ball.

"Take mine. My name is on it, but I doubt they will check."

Daisy's face lit up, then darkened again almost immediately. "I have nothing to wear."

"I have something."

Patrick was happy to pick out melodies on the piano while the women went to sift through Leontine's array of ball gowns. Leontine hoped he would allow her spend more time with him in that endeavor.

Daisy had never in her young life experienced the joy of trying on fine clothing. There were four suitable gowns to choose from and the feel of the satins, velvets, laces and chiffons and the sumptuousness of the dyes, beads, embroidery and appliqués seduced and pampered as did nothing she had ever known. She admitted to herself that, before this moment, she considered Leontine's obsession with clothing as something aligned with snobbery, pride or at the very least, self-indulgence. That assessment was at odds with her experience of her benefactor however, and she had, on some level, been attempting to make the preoccupation acceptable in her mind. That judgment was now laid to rest. She was more resolved than ever to ferret out the story promoted by Lilly White and convince Clarence Miller of her worthiness as a writer so that she might be able to elevate her income level and spend some well-earned cash at Trenwith's. The gown she selected was a light-coral taffeta trumpet-dress with fitted waist, ruched bodice and a daring square neckline lavishly adorned with a floral pattern of brick and cream-colored embroidery, sequins and chocolate-colored glass beads dangling from tiny delicate golden chains. The embroidery, sequins and beads were also generously affixed to the upturned hemline. Her cream-colored laced shoes were invisible under the long gown but the color was repeated in silk gloves that extended past each elbow. Leontine helped her freshen the chignon of her Gibson Girl hairstyle and secured the bouffant in place with bejeweled hairpins.

Daisy loved the look on Patrick's face when she went back into the living room to spin around for him. Leontine made her wait for a moment while she rushed back to her room to retrieve an atomizer filled with La Rose Jacquemino perfume and returned to give Daisy a light spritz at the wrist and neckline, and then another moment as she fetched her beaver cape with a loose fitting hood to ward off the evening chill of the coastline that inevitably set in once the sun went down no matter how warm the day.

Leontine and Patrick followed Daisy down the stairs to wait outside with her for one of the many carriages generously hired by Milo Potter to transport the citizenry to his hotel for this special evening. As they stood waiting in front of the market they discussed where best to focus the efforts of the other two while Daisy attended the ball. Reasoning that many of the characters they hoped to observe would be at the hotel whether or not they were attending the ball, they all decided it could prove fruitful to loiter in the lobby or perhaps the first floor gaming areas. If they were lucky Rear Admiral Haines or Captain John Adams might be milling around and willing to thrill a ten-year-old boy with tales of the sea. They decided it was worth a shot and in the end Leontine and Patrick joined Daisy in the carriage.

Patrick calculated that any officers attending the ball would have to take the elevator from their rooms. He suggested they plant themselves someplace between the elevator doors and the ballroom entrance with the intention of approaching the Admiral or the Captain – or both if the opportunity presented. His reasoning proved sound and in fairly short order Leontine recognized Rear Admiral Haines as he emerged from the elevator car. She gave Patrick a nudge. Had she not seen him repeatedly introduced at events around town, Leontine would never have guessed that this was the man in charge of the mighty fleet of ships and the thousands of sailors contained therein. He was small in stature and smaller in presence, eyes darting in a furtive manner. As Haines advanced along the corridor en route to the ballroom, Patrick stepped in front of him, snapped to attention, and executed a crisp salute, startling the man. He quickly recovered but the jolt annoyed him and he glowered down at the boy and nearly delivered a harsh reprimand to the child to stay out of his way. Once focusing on the sincere young lad before him, however, the Rear Admiral implemented a more military salute for young Patrick than he had managed for any of the crewmen under his command, though he was clearly ill at ease and at a loss for words.

"The ships are huge," Patrick gushed. "Bigger than anything!"

"They are," the Rear Admiral agreed as he finally wiped the scowl from his face. He studied Patrick for a moment, trying to come up with something pleasant to say to this earnest little boy.

"What's your name, Son?" Admiral Haines asked.

"Patrick Denman, Sir. I live in Santa Barbara."

Leontine stepped in to say, "It's all so thrilling, Admiral, as I'm sure you know. Patrick has spoken of nothing else for weeks."

Admiral Haines flicked his eyes to the woman, and then returned his attention to Patrick.

"Would you like to go aboard?" he asked.

Patrick did not have to pretend. "Yes, I would!"

"I'll arrange it," the Rear Admiral told Leontine, though he did not look directly at her as he spoke. "Leave your son's name at the front desk."

Leontine saw a young officer at his side make a note. She opened her mouth, about to explain that Patrick was not her son, but then saw no benefit and so, once more, let the impression stand uncorrected.

"Thank you, Admiral," she said, "You are very kind."

The admiral saluted Patrick once more, then headed in the direction of the ballroom. Others, taking their cue from Patrick, now approached the Admiral and Leontine suspected a man so reserved might come to regret that moment of big-heartedness.

"I'll leave your father's name," she murmured to Patrick. "The ships intimidate me even at this distance. I have no desire to see them up close."

The two of them waited around awhile hoping to have a chance to form an impression of Captain Adams, but it seemed he was not coming or, more likely, was already inside. They decided to leave the names at the front desk as instructed and in so doing passed a corridor where none other than Captain Adams and a most elegantly turned out Lilly White stood in animated conversation. She only caught a glimpse, but Leontine saw Lilly standing, hands on hips, chin thrust forward and eyes narrowed at Captain Adams who stood with his back against the wall. Leontine could think of more than one reason the young girl might have to lay into the Captain. She would have liked to pause just out of sight to see if she could hear something of their conversation but Patrick was already nearly to the front desk. She hurried on.

The conversation in the corridor was only partially as Leontine imagined. Lilly had been filling Captain Adams in on her conversation with Steven Magness and her meeting with Daisy. Adams was less than impressed with Lilly's choice of ally. Even her suggestion that Daisy might benefit them with influence stretching all the way to San Francisco did nothing to convince Adams that a newspaper*woman* was the best instrument to further their cause. He assumed Steven Magness would feel the same. Not wanting to poison his mood for the entire evening, Lilly suggested they head into the ballroom where perhaps a more suitable candidate would be found among the many reporters no doubt covering the ball. Captain Adams considered that a reasonable possibility, but then threw a wet blanket over the entire affair by informing Lilly they should keep their distance from one another once inside.

"We don't want to appear in collusion," he explained.

"Collusion," she repeated, fully suspicious he was holding back because of his wife. That's when her hands had gone to her hips. Never one to avoid confrontation, Lilly addressed the issue head on. "Will I find Elizabeth in the ballroom?"

"You will not."

"Then why not –" she began, but Adams held up his hand to stop her talking.

"Just pay attention to Magness. We need to reassure him. Settle him down."

She knew he was probably right, but that did not stop her from wanting to dance with him. Drink champagne with him. *Be* with him, especially in such a beautiful city and on such a beautiful night. Adams turned and strode from the corridor and Lilly had to take a moment to collect herself lest she make her grand entrance into the ballroom in tears.

Inside the celebration was even more magical than any could have anticipated. The formal ball to the officers of the fleet was the high point of the social festivities of the week and the Potter was transformed for the occasion into a virtual indoor garden. The massive pillars of the lobby were entwined with greenery, great festoons of flowers drooped from the ceilings and palms and vines hid the walls of the ballroom. All officers of the fleet from admirals to midshipmen were present, save those on active duty out in the channel. Glittering lights, draped fabrics and bushels of Lady Bankshire roses ornamented every corner of the spacious ballroom. At one end, opposite the far distant orchestra stand, stood black-draped tables supporting three champagne fountains and hundreds of fluted glasses made of crystal, delicate petit fours, tiny sandwiches and perfect strawberries, pears and pomegranates arranged on multi-tiered silver platters. Though many of the city's musicians had been playing much of the day they found a second wind in the festive atmosphere.

Local men were looking dapper with freshly trimmed mustaches, long tails, trim waistcoats, crisp stand-up collars and cravat neckties. Most had arrived in their best stovepipe hat, all now securely checked and resting on shelves in neat rows in the hotel cloakroom. Women in attendance had each spent hours in preparation for the ball. The opportunities for formal dress in Santa Barbara were few and far between, and the women played full out for the fleet ball. The room swirled in silk, satin, velvet, gems, jewels and sequins. The military men in attendance dazzled in full dress uniform with tails, deeply creased trousers, gilded buttons and epaulettes.

Rank and file crewmen meanwhile, rotated passes into the city itself, as their collective numbers would overwhelm the small town if too many came ashore at once. Local women attending dances on the Boulevard or venturing into the eating or even drinking establishments in town had spent no less time at their toilettes than the elegant ladies attending the ball, and what they lacked in adornment was more than made up for in enthusiasm.

Admiral Haines no sooner entered the ballroom than he was accosted by a reporter from the *Morning Press*. As determined as he was to impose upon himself the diction and bearing of high command, Haines became immediately frustrated by his lack of quick access to vocabulary which left him halting and stammering as he spoke. He was muddling through his first comment when he realized he had already lost his audience. The reporter was struggling to stay focused on his subject, but Haines saw the man's eyes flick over his head several times and then finally turned to see for himself what was tugging at the man's interest. To his utter annoyance he saw that it was Captain John Adams who had only just arrived. His stature and appearance seemed to outweigh the military hardware hanging on the front of Haines' uniform. The Rear Admiral stopped talking and the reporter did not even notice for several moments. When he did notice, he thanked the Admiral for his time and headed immediately in the direction of the Captain.

Resentment burned in Haines' chest. His eyes swept the room. He could see the ignorant women nearby attempting to gain the Captain's attention with transparent coquettish charms. He saw men near him stand taller and circle protective arms around their women. Haines wondered how long he should wait before he beat his retreat. He had never danced one step in his life and certainly would not start tonight. Let Adams command the party, he thought. It was the only attention he would garner – Haines would see to that. He looked around to see if he could spot Kurt Gunn. Apparently that gentleman had no interest in ballroom dancing either. Nor did Steven Magness, whom the Rear Admiral would have found still drinking in the first floor bar had he looked for him there.

Daisy circled the ballroom searching for Gunn as well. She watched Captain Adams enter and the subsequent swarm of admirers. She saw also the arrival of Lilly White who seemed out of sorts though ravishing in her party frock. Daisy headed in her direction.

"Miss White," Daisy said as she approached. "How nice to see you again."

"Thank you," the hostess said, "though you're turning out to be a bit of a hard sell I'm afraid. Captain Adams is not convinced you're up to the task of unmasking the conspiracy."

"I'm not convinced there *is* a conspiracy so don't trouble yourself on my account."

That comment stirred in Lilly White the determination to convince this woman that the Captain's cause was an important one, whether or not she would ultimately become the mouthpiece for revealing the treachery. Evil was afoot and Kurt Gunn was the source. The fact that Lilly did not herself fully understand exactly how John would benefit from this course of action did not in any way diminish the fervor with which she intended to pursue his objective. But what real male reporter could be secured if even this silly newsgirl remained unconvinced, she worried.

"I have seen no documents," Daisy reminded her. "Nor can I locate Kurt Gunn. I'm beginning to wonder if he exists at all. And I wonder as well, Miss White, how it is you will benefit by pulling the rug from under this corporate mischief."

"I won't benefit at all, nor would I seek to. And I would hardly describe it as mischief. Innocent people have been harmed, even killed because of these lies. Isn't that reason enough?"

Daisy shot back what was rapidly becoming her signature phrase, "We'll see."

The atmosphere was far too celebratory for serious investigative activity so after a short while Daisy decided to just relax and have some fun. For nearly two hours she chatted around the room and then danced with several of the naval officers in attendance. She had not spent much time dancing in her life to date and knew she was miserable at it, but if it didn't bother her partners she wasn't going to let it bother her. She spent several minutes in conversation with Patrick's father and his date, mostly for the sake of sheer snoopiness. Miss Chase was obviously well-known and well-liked and Daisy had to admit they made a likely couple, though she had noticed Patrick did not seem all that keen on her. When her feet finally wore out, Daisy went to rest on a padded bench in the lobby and found Charlie Peavey there fetching carriages for revelers who were ready to head home. She queued up and when her turn came he helped her climb into a seat with the utmost care and attention. Daisy thanked him sincerely and, as the driver set the horses in motion, considered what she might say to him if he ever worked up enough courage to ask if he might call on her.

Chapter I4

At eight the following morning, Daisy left her office and took the
trolley back to the Potter Hotel. Youthful anatomy allowed for her to
carry on with only the three hours of sleep she had stolen between the
dance and reporting for typesetting duties at four a.m. Setting the myriad
accounts of the excitement from the previous day made her aware that
she had been engrossed enough in the intrigue of corporate pirates and
military villains that she had failed to fully absorb any of the momentous
occasions of the preceding few days. She had not even attempted her own
written account. It is the nature of the optimist however, to embrace the
world as it is, and so Daisy thought to herself, *"All the better,"* and
reasoned that her time should not be wasted on obvious and pedestrian
news telling. She had a much bigger fish on the line and her boss would
soon know about it.

As she had anticipated, the desk clerk at the Potter was not particularly accommodating about providing information concerning the
elusive Mr. Gunn. He did acknowledge that Daisy's written note had been
delivered to his room, but could not say whether he had shown up to find
it. Nor would he speculate as to the gentleman's current whereabouts.
Daisy went to the elevator and stood deep in thought tapping her teeth
with her pen. If the military men had commandeered the fifth floor, it
stood to reason that the next most illustrious guests would be found in the
next most illustrious quarters - fourth floor, ocean view. How many rooms
could there possibly be? Upon exiting the elevator on the fourth floor,
Daisy padded around the corridors and quickly realized there were many

more rooms than she had imagined. As she wandered the hallways, Daisy passed one of the hotel maids so many times that the woman began to feel uneasy about it. The maid was relieved in a way when the strange girl finally poked her head into the room she was cleaning to solicit her help.

"Hello? You there!" Daisy called to the braided, blue-eyed maid. "I'm looking for Mr. Kurt Gunn. Do you know, is he in his room?"

Most of the women on the Potter housekeeping staff were Scandinavian, many very recent arrivals, who lived in the dormitory wing at the back the of hotel. Though of Danish heritage and appearance, this particular maid had come from nowhere more exotic than Los Angeles however, where she had also worked for Milo Potter at his Hotel Van Nuys.

"I'm sorry, Miss, we are not told the names of the guests. Perhaps you could just knock on his door?"

Well, so much for that. Daisy thanked the maid and then rode the elevator down to the main second floor as she tried to conjure her next move. She went back to the lobby where she spotted a clot of bejeweled dowagers heading out to the sun porch. In the absence of a plan she decided to follow her instincts and she tailed the women into the sunny room.

"Excuse me," she said, as the women chose seats and motioned for hotel staff to situate them here or there at this or that angle as they fingered their jewelry and arranged their hats against the sun. "I'm looking for my brother, Kurt Gunn. Do any of you know him?"

None of them did. Daisy repeated this exchange with every soul she encountered inside and outside the hotel and found no one who even knew who he was. By the time she finished her canvassing the lack of sleep was beginning to take a toll and she ultimately decided that the best course of action for her at this particular juncture was to go back home and take a nap.

Meanwhile, Rear Admiral Haines was in his room running over his speech in his mind that would be delivered in due course to a group of successful entrepreneurs at The Santa Barbara Club on Figueroa Street at Chapala. He did not know the benefit of rehearsing the physical formation and utterance of the trite and obvious words he had chosen, which doomed the delivery of his uninspired message that much more.

There on the fifth floor, Captain Adams, Rear Admiral Haines and his Ensign, Darrell Stroud, had taken a suite of rooms connected by an interior corridor. Only Haines' room had direct access to the exterior hallway. As he silently went over the talking points in his speech he paused, suddenly aware that an argument was taking place in the next room – Captain Adams' room. Elizabeth Adams had shown up at her husband's quarters to ask for one afternoon of attention for their son. He would be gone in three day's time and it did not seem outlandish for him to give over a few short hours, whatever his workload might be. It irked her to even have to ask, and her husband's response had enraged her. She took Quincy into the interior hallway to wait, not wanting him to see her upset and had then returned to Adams' room to have it out with him about the situation once and for all.

"I have too much on my mind," he growled. "How dare you come to me with this now!"

"He's your son," she hissed, and saw his lip curl in distaste at the reminder. "Will you deprive him of even one moment of joy?"

"I said don't bother me with this. Just keep him away from me."

Elizabeth went silent for a moment, rage boiling in her chest.

"Your shame is misplaced, John. You should feel it for yourself."

"Get out of my sight!"

And then she raised her own voice. "You will never have what you want! I'll sue for divorce! Good luck with your politics then!"

Out in the corridor, Quincy could hear the anger and desperation in his mother's voice. He had no attachment to the man inside and his one thought, if it was a thought at all, was to get to his mother's side. Quincy began to wail and kick at the Captain's door with all his might. The sounds drew Admiral Haines to his door, the escalating nature of the apparent argument causing him to look around quickly for a weapon. His glance landed on a heavy glass ashtray in a clunky wooden base beautifully etched with the words "Potter Hotel". He and Captain Adams jerked their doors open at nearly the same instant.

Quincy flew at his father and landed several painful kicks to his legs. Adams tried to grab his son's flailing arms but when he finally managed to grab hold of the giant, frantic boy, Quincy sunk his teeth into Adams' hand between his thumb and index finger. Adams howled in pain. He struck the boy in the head and sent him sprawling on the floor. It wasn't the violence that pushed Percifal Haines over the edge. It was the look of revulsion, the disgust that replaced the rage on John Adams' face when he looked at his son. That look loosed a cascade of a thousand bitter moments stored in the Rear Admiral's mind like tiny flames igniting a molten pool of resentment deep in his body.

Haines did not remember closing the distance to the other officer's doorway. He had no picture in his mind of how he dived at the Captain, how he swung the ashtray with all his might, crushing the windpipe of the much bigger and younger man. He didn't realize he had dropped the makeshift weapon to the floor and fallen on the already dying man, straddling his body and wrapping his hands around his throat, though the ashtray had already done the job. Adams clutched and clawed, insane in his desperation for air but Haines' hands were locked in a vice-like grip and in less than a minute more, Captain John Adams was dead.

When Admiral Haines regained the ability to see and hear he was looking into the terrified eyes of Elizabeth Adams. The Captain lay still beneath him, eyes forever staring. His wife's hands had come to her mouth to stifle a scream that never materialized, paralyzed with confusion, fear and disbelief.

Haines turned his head but closed his eyes, not able to face what he could feel beneath his body. He felt dizzy. He felt sick – oh God, he was going to be sick! His eyes flew open on their own to stop the spinning and keep from vomiting and he looked directly into the sightless eyes of John Adams, his face contorted as he died fighting for breath. Haines rolled onto the floor unable to think or reason. He felt nauseous again. He went to his hands and knees thinking to crawl someplace where he could be sick in peace. He tried to slow his breathing, to get a sense of what was happening. After a few moments he looked again at Elizabeth Adams. She was staring at the lifeless form of her husband, her expression unreadable.

She was actually thinking that this was not such a horrible turn of events. Her husband's pension would provide for his family as well as he ever had and in truth the role of grieving widow was a step up from pitiable abandoned wife. She felt calm, much more calm than she had before this surreal turn of events.

Rear Admiral Haines and Elizabeth Adams never spoke a word, yet they came to several agreements in the space of a few moments; first that she would take her son and flee, second, that Haines would deal with the room in some way, and finally, that neither of them would say a word. Elizabeth did not look at her husband again. She drew one ragged breath, then composed herself completely and left the room to comfort her son and leave the hotel as quickly as possible.

It had seemed an eternity but in actuality fewer than ten minutes had elapsed from the time Quincy began kicking the door to when his father lay dead on the floor. Haines began to shake uncontrollably, his teeth chattering. He had yet to regain the ability to reason. Everything he did in the next two minutes was accomplished in a trance-like state. He left the body as it was. He wiped the ashtray with his shirt and replaced it on the floor, then ransacked the room making it appear someone had been looking for something. He locked the door between their rooms from Adams' side and then slipped quickly into his own room by the door opening into the interior corridor.

Once in his own room Haines was overwhelmed by the enormity of what had just happened. He felt he would fly apart. He had to get out of this room, this proximity, but felt so completely out of control there was no way he could behave normally. He paced maniacally back and forth, his mind spinning but with no coherent thought. But then the movement began to have a calming effect. His heart was no longer racing, his breath slowed to normal and he could feel the sweat on the back of his neck begin to evaporate. He was through it, through the panic of it and the ability to think returned.

Reclaiming that ability however, rapidly became a curse. It was survival he told himself first. But, no, he had been in no danger. Not only that, he had not truly feared for the life of the Mongoloid child. He had taken enough whippings in his young years to know the boy was not badly harmed. What then? How could this horrific act be defended? If it could not be then he was a killer and was duty bound to turn himself in.

It was an accident. God knows he had not intended to kill the man, only to come to the aid of a child. It was an accident, that's all. He should call someone immediately and confess. His mind calculated the probable outcome of that course of action in less than a second. It would mean his career, without question, and probably his freedom. Perhaps even his life.

Self-preservation is an elemental aspect of human nature and will arise unbidden and fully flowered when necessary. It painted the event in a softer hue, dimmed the light of stark reality and brought with it something calming and reasoning and clear from the depths of his psyche. Justification. He had been justified in his actions. One might know the term "blind rage" and even believe they understand what it means, but to live through the experience of it is another matter entirely. He realized now that if he replayed the sequence of events in his mind he had no visual record between the time he saw Captain Adams strike his son and when he regained his senses looking into the eyes of Elizabeth Adams. He had no memory of how he had come to be straddling the man on the floor. No memory of the feel of the heavy ashtray shattering the tissue inside the man's throat. Why should his own life be forfeit when he had been virtually unconscious at the time and therefore helpless to affect the sequence of events? Admiral Haines suspected that this internal tug-of-war was far from over and also that he should delay making any decisions until he had thought it through fully. Whatever the ultimate outcome, there were a dozen crucial actions to be taken immediately. The worst thing he could do was hide in his room next door to the catastrophe. He needed instantaneous physical distance and more importantly, an alibi. He needed to be seen somewhere now, before the body was discovered.

Haines left through the door to the exterior hallway, forced himself to walk slowly and pressed the call button for the elevator. When the car arrived a minute later it was empty, a stroke of random luck that Haines took as a sign he was proceeding on the correct path. He sunk rapidly to the first floor and made eye contact with as many people as he could on his way to the game room. He smiled at everyone, even clapping the shoulder of a young officer who had made a good throw on the bowling alley. His behavior was so out of character that many in proximity would recall his presence there when they later learned of the tragedy that had occurred five stories above their heads.

* * *

It was nearly two hours before an unfortunate member of the housekeeping staff discovered the body. Haines was near the veranda, heading out to the street to take his place in a motorcar that would deliver him to the Santa Barbara Club. It was Milo Potter himself who whispered in the Rear Admiral's ear. Haines motioned to Captain Nicholson of the

USS *Alabama*, quickly ordering him to take his place in the automobile. The officer saluted and did as commanded.

In the intervening hours a realization had come to Percifal Haines. He at last recognized the importance of something so simple and yet so immense it was incredible he had not grasped its significance earlier. He had all the power. This recognition had changed Rear Admiral Haines immediately. Quite suddenly the men in his command were behaving much more as Haines had always imagined they should. He was unaware that it was a reflection of his own internal shift. The events of the day had changed the way he moved, the way he spoke, even the way he thought. In the effort to appear normal and act the part of a commanding officer he had inadvertently achieved a success that had long eluded him. He was now completely in control. It was exhilarating. He followed Milo Potter to the scene of the crime. The housekeeper who had made the discovery was standing outside the door in the interior hallway terrified and in tears. Her English was sparse however and Danny Ordaz went looking for someone to interpret her horrific account.

Rear Admiral Haines was quick to take control of the situation. He looked at the corpse and was amazed at the detachment he felt from the truth. He immediately began an orchestration of events that would allow him to acquire all the knowledge he would need to steer the investigation away from himself. When Milo Potter made the obvious suggestion to notify the police, Admiral Haines agreed but immediately made clear how their involvement would be viewed.

"It's a military matter. I will take charge of the investigation."

Milo Potter was in no great rush to have the tragedy known. It would be a terrible thing to overlay the community celebration with this horror, and though he would never say it out loud, it could be very bad for business. He was more than willing to go along. Haines began barking orders at everyone in the room.

"Transport the body to the *Constitution*. Immediately. Ship's doctor will conduct the autopsy. Send someone to notify the police chief. And tell him I want to see him. And send me my Ensign," he commanded and then headed to his own room without a backward glance at the grisly scene behind him.

Chapter 15

James Ross, the Chief of Police for the City of Santa Barbara had more on his plate than he could deal with at the moment. He was wallowing in the aftermath of a near-riot that had erupted the night before at John Senich's Oyster Café on State Street. Several of the visiting crewmen claimed their bill had been artificially inflated. Great offense was taken at the assertion, not only by the accurately accused Mr. Senich, but by half a dozen liquor-fueled locals as well. Quite a lot of damage was done to the café, but Chief Ross was pretty sure Mr. Senich probably got what he deserved. Fourteen men had been lectured soundly and sent home to sleep it off. He sent a couple of them up to St. Francis Hospital but all they did was clean them up a little bit and send them home as well. No sooner had the worn out officer finally gone home to bed than he was rousted from his slumber to intervene in an altercation on Nopal Street that saw two neighbors holding each other at gun point over a political argument run wild. By the time he had sorted it all out and wrested the firearms from the ultimately sheepish men, a new day of busy policing had already begun. Chief Ross knew he needed to prepare for more of the same in the ensuing days and as a consequence, he asked the county sheriff, Nat Stewart to deal with whatever was happening at the Potter Hotel as a personal favor.

Nat Stewart was a more than decent lawman and he had a bad feeling about the handling of the confounding event at the Potter Hotel right from the start. The sheriff was a calm man by nature, slow to rile, but once done he usually won the day with whatever situation he was forced to resolve at the time. He lived at 319 East Anapamu Street with his wife Mary who was currently deeply embroiled in the planning of their daughter Elsie's upcoming nuptials in June. This particular afternoon was her second attempt at entertaining their future son-in-law's parents in their home, the first effort having been thwarted by Stewart's omnipresent duties as local law enforcement. In her view nothing Chief Ross had in the offing could be more important than the approaching tea time and she was none too happy with her husband for accepting the task of reporting to the beachfront.

Stewart showed up at the Potter with the coroner, Antonio Ruiz, as fast as he could get there. It had been something less than an hour since he learned of the tragedy, yet when he arrived he found the body had already been removed and was informed the victim was bound for the U.S.S. *Constitution* for autopsy. That didn't sit right. He left Ruiz to look over the murder scene and went to talk to Rear Admiral Haines in the adjoining room. Sheriff Stewart disliked Haines immediately. He didn't like the way the Admiral assumed control and he didn't like his condescending attitude. Were the city not so swollen with visitors and invigorated locals it would not be happening like this, but he had to acknowledge that, after all, the man was an Admiral in the United States Navy. The fact was, Stewart didn't have time for this any more than the police chief did and knew he should be counting his blessings that the military was willing to shoulder the entire burden of investigating the crime.

"I will conduct inquiries here," the Rear Admiral told the lawman. "You'll be informed if I need assistance."

Irritating, but the sheriff would win nothing but more work for himself if he challenged the authority of this visiting officer.

"There's a wife here in town. I'll see her myself," Haines added. It wouldn't do to have anyone talking to Elizabeth Adams before he had a chance to verify that their silent pact was real and intact.

The offer took the edge off Stewart's aversion to the man. The widow would no doubt appreciate that the Rear Admiral himself was taking an interest in her personal tragedy. There seemed to be nothing else to do at the moment besides offering up whatever assistance was wanted or needed and then getting out of the way. He should make it home well in time to satisfy his wife.

Once alone in his room, Rear Admiral Haines had a moment for reflection. A course of action had been chosen, that was now clear. The crime would be covered up. He checked inside to see if he could live with that and was gratified to find the flower of justification opening ever wider in his soul. It would be devastating for the citizenry to learn of such a crime at a time like this. Even more devastating to the officers and crewmen of the fleet. It was unthinkable that they should lose three commanding officers in less than two weeks, first Rear Admiral Evans, then the Captain, then himself. And what had been lost, really? A strutting narcissist. An opportunist. A sterling example of the immorality that had become the contemporary norm. Haines' mind was at peace; he was doing the right thing. He took a sheet of notepaper emblazoned with a drawing of the Potter Hotel and bent to make a thoughtful list of characters that might possibly need to be managed. Steven Magness, of course, and Kurt Gunn. Haines did not know who all was aware of the corporate conspiracy but he had some ideas about where to start looking. It was the perfect framework as motive for murder. Lilly White could be a problem. Yet, because she was young and female and therefore foolish by his estimation, she might well be the easiest tool of manipulation. He even wondered if he dare implicate her as a suspect and the thought made him smirk. Haines dropped a note in Ensign Stroud's room instructing him to locate those three individuals and deliver them for interrogation as soon as he returned from delivering the body to the ship.

* * *

Danny heard plenty from the house and kitchen staff. Helge Swensen, the young woman who found the body, told him through an interpreting English-speaking maid, about something one of the maids had said earlier in the day about a woman acting strangely and looking for a man on the fourth floor whose name the maid could not remember. From the description Danny knew immediately that Daisy Merrie was the woman she had seen. Anticipating she would face more questioning at some point as the one who stumbled upon the body, Miss Swensen asked Danny if she should divulge Daisy's actions to the Rear Admiral. Danny reasoned that it was very unlikely the two events were even related and advised Miss Swensen to leave Daisy out of it.

At his lunch break Danny caught the trolley to State Street and disembarked in front of the Birabent Market. He found Leontine inside behind the register, the account book open in front of her.

"I wonder if you can keep the biggest secret of the century," he said as he faced his cousin over the counter.

Leontine closed the ledger, titillated by the opening. "Of course."

Danny checked over each shoulder to make certain they would not be overheard by a young mother pinching fruit with one hand while she rocked her baby in a wicker carriage with the other.

"There's been a murder," he murmured. "A murder at the Potter Hotel."

Leontine gasped and her hand went to her heart.

"It's worse than that," Danny continued. "It was one of the captains. The one with a family here."

"John Adams."

Danny nodded. He looked around again and then related the true nature of his business. "I talked to one of the maids not fifteen minutes ago. The poor soul who found the body."

"How dreadful!" Leontine imagined the horror of making such a discovery.

"She said Daisy was snooping around and acting strange and she wondered if it was related to the death. If she had that idea the Admiral might also. I told her not to say anything – but what if she does? Leontine, do you know what's going on?"

"Not at all, but I suddenly very much want to talk to Daisy."

* * *

Steven Magness was passed out in his room. He had spent another sleepless night and in sheer desperation began drinking again at mid-morning in an attempt to render himself unconscious. He was finally sleeping heavily when the Ensign came to his door shortly after the lunch hour, and it took some time for the knocking of the insistent Ensign to penetrate the density of his unconsciousness. Magness finally responded to the pounding on the door that matched the pounding beginning in his head. He was irritable and disagreeable with the young officer so intent on delivering him to his commanding officer for a reason he would not disclose. Magness was angry enough to refuse him. What right did the military have to command a civilian, he could have challenged. But he was too sick and too tired. It would be over sooner if he just went along. He made the Ensign wait outside the door while he tugged at his rumpled clothing and then stared stupidly at himself for a full minute in the mirror affixed above a chest of drawers in his room. Finally he stepped into the bathroom and splashed a little water on his face, smeared his hair down as best he could with wet hands and then went into the hallway to follow the sailor up one flight of stairs to the fifth floor.

Magness would have liked to remain standing once inside the Rear Admiral's room, a trick he had used in countless corporate office confrontations and negotiations, to create a bit of tension and throw the balance in the room off-kilter. He wasn't up to the task just now however, and he eased into an incongruously stylish chair across from a utilitarian desk the hotel had graciously moved into the Rear Admiral's suite. A four-panel, folding wooden screen had been erected to separate the makeshift office area from the bed and armoire. An artistic rendering of silhouetted trees at sunset was repeated in each of the panels of the room divider and though a handsome piece, it obscured the far more lovely view through the window of the Potter grounds and the Channel Islands beyond the fleet of ships bobbing in the waters in between. It was all lost on Steven Magness in any case as it was all he could do to stare grumpily at the naval officer shuffling paper on his desk and wait for him to state his business.

Haines began, "Captain John Adams was found murdered in his room earlier today. What can you tell me about that?"

Magness' eyes widened and he gaped at the irritating man across the desk in disbelief for several moments. "What do you mean, murdered?"

"I know exactly who you are - and I know what you need."

"What I need? I don't know what you're talking about."

"I think you do. And you should know you are the first person I am interviewing. My gut tells me I need look no further for the Captain's killer. Where were you between ten and eleven o'clock this morning?"

"Downstairs in the bar and then in my room," Magness admitted. "But, how was he…how did he die?"

Haines did not for one second alter his accusatory stance even in the face of such a seemingly clear alibi.

"I'm ordering you to remain available for questioning." That time Haines heard it himself. His voice was lower, he felt it in his chest. It caused him to sit up a little taller.

"You order me?" Internally Magness had already made the decision to flee. Nothing good could come of this. Adams was dead, at least three people he knew of could connect them and alibi or no this whole unsavory business was likely to cook his goose. To say nothing of the damning report that now seemed destined to see daylight.

"You are to remain here at the hotel," Haines ordered.

"If you say so."

Haines narrowed his eyes at Magness as he left the room. Surprisingly he found he actually harbored suspicion about the man. Now how could that be knowing, as he did without question, that Magness was innocent? Remarkable.

He summoned his Ensign to retrieve the next person for initial questioning. He found he enjoyed this preliminary exchange and the opportunity to observe the unguarded reaction of "suspects" to the news of his own colossal misdeed. He considered altering his instruction to the Ensign with regard to the hostess. He had initially been dreading his interview with Lilly White and instructed his Ensign to break the news to her. The last thing he wanted to witness was the thrashing and wailing of a heartbroken debutante. Let her get that out of her system before he had her in front of him. Upon further consideration he let that order stand. The Ensign informed him that Kurt Gunn was nowhere to be found. It seemed he had checked into his room and then simply disappeared. Haines decided this would be good use of the local police force, to set them looking for Gunn. It would make them feel necessary and included he reasoned, and keep them out of his business. He directed the Ensign in that regard and instructed him also to send in the first on a list of hotel staff members and guests.

Chapter 16

Leontine observed Daisy attempting to keep the excitement she felt at bay. Of course it would be exhilarating for the girl to find herself neck deep in such sordid business, Leontine thought. She is a writer after all. The two women sat at the kitchen table trying to come to terms with such a dastardly development and discussing the best course of action. Danny had told Leontine that their cousin, Coroner Antonio Ruiz, had been very upset that the body was removed so quickly and questioned the decision to go along made by Sheriff Stewart. Leontine wondered now what she and Daisy could possibly do, and if they should do anything at all.

"We have to! This is much bigger than anything we imagined. It's up to us – you can see that, can't you?"

Reluctantly, Leontine had to agree. Somehow they had stumbled into the middle of a murderous maze and now they had no other recourse than to ferret their way out. As they spoke they heard the grind of the doorbell below. Leontine knew it was Patrick, having scheduled – not a lesson – but some time to play the piano together. Patrick seemed to have a natural ability for music and she wanted to see where it went before she imposed conventional structure.

Leontine said, "I don't know if we should tell him what's happened."

"Are you crazy? We need his brains!"

And it was Daisy that jumped up to let him in.

Once they began to fill Patrick in on what they knew they quickly realized they did not know much at all. Only that Lilly White and the one businessman seemed to be allied with the unfortunate Captain while the Captain's boss and the other businessman were against him.

"You said his wife was pretty miserable," Daisy offered.

"Yes," Leontine replied, "but I can't imagine her killing the man no matter how unhappy her marriage."

Both women turned to Patrick to get his take on the matter.

He asked, "How did they kill him?"

Leontine and Daisy looked at each other. They didn't know.

Patrick went on. "Because if somebody bashed him in the head or stabbed him in the chest it was probably a man, but if they shot him or gave him some poison or something then it could have been a girl."

Reasonable.

"I think we're gonna need my dad," he concluded.

"And Sheriff Stewart if we're to learn any details," Leontine added.

Leontine was acquainted with Sheriff Stewart. He had been in office at the time of the death of her father and disappearance of Vincent Barón, and though he had not investigated the sad event as criminal, he had been as helpful as was possible in the ensuing years as Leontine attempted to unravel the mystery. When she found the remains of an overnight camp near the Indian Orchard ranch on San Marcos Road he had sent two deputies to investigate. And again when a broken shovel led her to what they all feared was a crude grave. If something had been buried there however, it had subsequently been retrieved at some point in time. Leontine tried hard not to abuse the lawman's better nature and was grateful for his seemingly endless compassion.

Nevertheless, the three now agreed that Daisy would be the one to find the sheriff, though they were unacquainted, and convince him to meet with them at Dr. Denman's office as soon as possible.

The Eddy Building at 808 State Street next to the County National Bank just above De la Guerra Street contained primarily professional offices. The tenants included several physicians, most of whom were specialists of some sort including an osteopath, a general surgeon and one devoted to injuries and malformations of the hands and feet. Dr. Denman's upstairs office had a small examination room entered through a relatively spacious receiving area and waiting room that contained half a dozen straight backed wooden chairs, his roll top desk with its copious nooks stuffed with papers, implements and medical objects, his wooden filing drawers for notes and patient records and a locking glass cabinet that held a modest supply of medicines he prescribed most often to save his clientele the trouble of going to The Gutierrez Drug Store two blocks away in the Fithian Building or the Sterling Drug Store even farther down State Street. Typically Nicholas manned the office alone, but there were times when he would hire the assistance of a qualified nurse if a sizeable catastrophe or widespread illness found him overwhelmed with patients. The week of the visiting fleet was such a time and when Leontine and Patrick entered the doctor's office they found the waiting room full and a hearty and robust nurse in severely starched whites with a commanding yet reassuring demeanor seated at the roll-top desk, tending to the patients she could or soothing the nerves of those who needed to wait to see the doctor in the examination room. Leontine hung back and let Patrick explain who he was and that he needed a few minutes with his father. Even those in obvious discomfort could not deny the request of a young boy for his father and as soon as a man with his arm in a sling stepped gingerly from the examination room Patrick and Leontine were allowed to proceed inside next.

Nicholas Denman was not eager to get involved in the sordid affair however. He was knee deep in the ill effects of citywide drunkenness – mostly stitches and compresses for victims of fighting and falling, but a few of the injuries were serious. The sailors seemed quite taken with many of the local girls, and vice-versa, but local boys were defending their own in ways that often ended up with someone visiting the doctor.

"Why on earth do you want to get involved with any of this?" he asked Leontine. "I'm not sure it's something I want around my son."

"I hope you don't think I would do anything to harm Patrick," she protested, trying to keep her voice from bristling but was not entirely certain she succeeded.

"Dad -- " Patrick started, but Leontine interrupted him to continue.

"I'll honor your decision, of course, Dr. Denman, if you have no interest in helping. I apologize if I've done anything to earn your disapproval."

Nicholas ran his hand through his hair. He looked over at his son who stood, arms crossed, glaring at him. He looked at his son's odd choice for a friend, this attractive but disconcerting woman, who probably would have been glaring, too, had she allowed herself to do it.

He sighed. "I don't know what you think I can do."

Patrick jumped at the opening, sensing that his father was caving in already.

"Danny, my friend at the Potter, said they sent the body out to the ship and it made the sheriff mad. I didn't tell you yet, but we get to go out there. You and me. To the ship. Miss Birabent already put your name at the desk to take me," he reported excitedly.

A little grin crept onto Leontine's face at Patrick's description of her cousin Danny as his friend. Nicholas raised an eyebrow.

"We want you to look at the body. We have to know how he got killed."

Nicholas drew in a long breath, thinking. "It's a big ship, Son. Do I just climb on board and ask if I can see the murdered Captain?"

Leontine told him, "Daisy is on her way here with Sheriff Stewart, as soon as she finds him that is. Perhaps he can be of some help in that regard."

Nicholas gave in fully then. "All right," he agreed, "I'll do what I can."

The look on Patrick's face suddenly seemed reason enough to become embroiled in this most unsettling affair.

After a dozen inquires in town, Daisy had finally located Nat Stewart breaking up an altercation in Angelo Miratti's saloon at 534 State Street. He had no more room in his jailhouse at the moment though and so was sending two lads to nurse their bloody noses and swelling eyes at home. He had to admit to some measure of relief that this excitable young newspaper girl was giving him good reason to delve more deeply into the events from earlier at the Potter Hotel. The whole scenario still bothered him and he had been trying to decide what to do about it. According to Daisy Merrie the thing to do was accompany her to Dr. Nicholas Denman's office up the street and have her fill him in on what she knew on the way.

Once they were all together the plotting and planning began in earnest. After deciding how best to proceed on so many fronts simultaneously they agreed to come back together at seven o'clock at the Potter to compare findings and reassess.

Leontine went back to the market. She knew everyone involved wanted to keep the story quiet and she understood that from several angles. Nonetheless, she had decided to confide in her Uncle Remi. He had a true and simple heart and Leontine relied on him more than he knew. She was to contact Elizabeth Adams but was having difficulty coming up with a reason to do so.

"Awful business. Who broke the news to her?" Remi asked.

"I don't know. One of the officers I suppose. Or Mr. Potter."

"Let's deliver some flowers," he suggested. "A bereavement bouquet, courtesy of the United States Navy."

Brilliant!

Leontine rented a small horse carriage from the Tally Ho, thankfully this time hitched up to her favorite mare, Lindy Sue, purchased a beautiful arrangement of flowers from Mrs. Halmer's flower stand on East Haley Street, gathered her nerve and then went in search of the new widow. As Lindy Sue clopped along the hard-packed dirt of Santa Barbara Street she moved her hat further forward on her head to catch a bit of an ocean breeze on the back of her neck. She had selected her navy wool suit dress with an unadorned hat befitting the somber task before her and though appropriate, it was uncomfortably warm in the early afternoon sun.

Leontine found the home at 107 East Micheltorena Street with no trouble. Her approach revealed the clean and clipped appearance of Mrs. Adams' small cottage. Even recently fallen leaves from a spreading magnolia tree dared not find themselves outside strictly squared-off sections of flower bed. If the landscaping was meticulously clear of debris, it was equally free of decorative flowers or even shrubbery. The south facing wooden porch and railing were painted and perfect. She reflected how often those whose lives were chaotic and out of control seemed to preserve some internal illusion of order by maintaining tidy surroundings. She left the carriage at the side of the road not bothering to tether Lindy Sue. She wouldn't go anywhere.

Leontine approached the front door and then stood for several moments with her hand raised, preparing to knock, as she tried to come up with at least a rough idea of what she was going to say. Once she did knock Mrs. Adams appeared in short order. As soon as she saw the flowers it seemed Mrs. Adams understood the purpose of the visit. She glanced over her shoulder and then stepped out onto the porch pulling the door closed behind her. Leontine passingly noticed that the woman was not wearing black.

"Mrs. Adams," Leontine began, "please forgive my intrusion."

Elizabeth Adams studied Leontine for a moment, vague signs of recognition fluttering across her face.

"We spoke the other morning on the Potter grounds. My son was looking for his whistle in the garden there."

"Of course," Elizabeth replied.

Leontine offered the flowers to the woman.

"The fleet contacted my store and asked that we communicate their most sincere condolences. I'm very sorry for your loss."

Elizabeth Adams locked eyes with Leontine as she reached for the flowers. "The fleet," she repeated.

There was something distrustful and steely in her gaze. It unnerved Leontine and she lost the ability to continue the masquerade.

"Actually, no. I'm so sorry. I learned of the death of your husband myself. My cousin is a manager at the hotel. I was touched having so recently seen you and your son and I just wanted to…." Her voice trailed off. The suspicion abated, but the steel beneath it remained.

"Come in," Mrs. Adams said.

The two women sat at Elizabeth Adams' kitchen table. It was a bright morning but the magnolia tree allowed very little sunlight to filter through the kitchen window and it left the room feeling utilitarian and cold. Quincy sat on the floor at their feet playing with toy farm animals carved from wood that had wheels for feet. He made quite a racket but the sounds were joyful and so somehow not disturbing to Leontine. They did seem to grate on her hostess however.

"It's unbearably shocking," Leontine remarked as she watched the boy play. "You must be devastated."

Mrs. Adams drew circles on the table with the bottom of her teacup. She did not look at Leontine as she spoke. "Yes, I am."

But Leontine did not believe her.

"They want to keep it quiet," Elizabeth added.

"Understandable, I suppose."

"He was killed you know. Someone killed him," the widow said, as if reminding herself of the fact.

"Yes," Leontine agreed. And then decided to just ask the question. "Who could do such a thing?"

Elizabeth Adams looked Leontine in the eye.

"I don't know," she replied.

But again, Leontine did not believe her.

* * *

Lilly did not know how much time had passed since she took to her bed. There was no time any more. Only a sinking, sickening weight in her chest and endless, searing hot tears of grief and loss and disappointment. She had twice refused a summons from Admiral Haines. She could not stand. She could not speak. She could only cry. Her aunt came by once with a promise to be nearby and then left her in solitude to get through the worst of it. As if she ever could. Why…who…she would start to wonder. And then her thoughts would collapse in a heap again, and she would weep again inconsolably.

Daisy had been informed by the desk clerk that Miss White was not answering any calls but offered to hold a message for her if Daisy cared to write one. She declined and was now making her way to the bar on the first floor. She would look for Steven Magness and, as always, for Kurt Gunn. When she entered the lounge it was Lilly's Aunt Anne she found however, and she made her way over to her table.

She said, "I don't know if you remember me, Daisy Merrie, *Daily News*. We met in the dining room."

"I remember." Anne did not offer Daisy a seat. Nevertheless, Daisy took one.

"I wonder if you know where I might find your niece. I very much need to speak with her."

Anne raised an elegant cocktail to her lips and took a long, slow drink. She looked Daisy in the eye over the rim of the glass, but did not reply.

"I can help her," Daisy pressed. She didn't know how much to say but she was pretty sure this woman knew about the Captain. Why else would she be acting so dark and strange?

Anne took another long drink. "I don't know how," she finally responded.

"I'd like to see if she'll talk to me. She might want to."

"She's in room 440. You can see if she answers."

In less than ten minutes Daisy was in the corridor outside the room.

She tapped lightly and called to Lilly through the door. She wanted to say why she was there but didn't dare until she was inside lest someone overhear. She waited twice as long as she thought reasonable and then finally headed reluctantly for the elevator when she heard someone call her name. She returned immediately to room 440 and found Lilly holding the door open a bit as she stood behind it in her room. Daisy had barely shut the door when Lilly began shrieking accusations that were nearly unintelligible through hysterical sobbing.

"It was Haines!" she screeched. "He hated John – he was jealous!" Daisy moved to Lilly, her body language encouraging the distraught girl in the direction of a chair.

"Maybe so," she replied calmly as she maneuvered the young woman into the chair, "but he's a high ranking officer. It doesn't make sense that he would kill one of his own in the very next room."

Lilly leapt to her feet again, unable to contain a firestorm of anger welling up inside her. "Then it was *her*," she raged. "Elizabeth – she made his life hell! She couldn't keep him so she killed him!"

"I suppose it's possible. I plan to talk to her about that."

Lilly paced maniacally, muttering to herself what she might do to Elizabeth Adams if she had the woman in front of her.

"But what about Kurt Gunn?" Daisy asked. "He had more reason than the others to have the Captain out of his way."

Lilly's eyes went wide. "Yes! He killed John. He acts like a saint but I know he's the devil!" She continued her frenetic activity, mumbling and pacing, eyes wild. Lilly was actually starting to give Daisy the creeps and as interesting as these spontaneous theories were, they were not really getting them anywhere.

"Do you want to find out for certain? Because if you do, we could use your help."

The appeal seemed to snap Lilly out of her hysteria. She blinked and looked around her almost as if mystified at where she was and with whom. And then Daisy watched as it all washed over her again and Lilly sank into the chair, buried her face in her hands and wept.

* * *

While Daisy was busy with Lilly White, Patrick and Nicholas took the trolley to the Potter with the intention of making good on Admiral

Haines' offer of a visit to the ship. They had no way of knowing whether the Admiral had informed anyone of the grand offer but it made sense to try any means to gain access to the body.

Meanwhile, Sheriff Stewart made his way to see the Admiral and impose some privileges befitting his station as the representative of the law of the land.

"I want to examine the deceased," he explained to Haines once he was in front of him. "I have reports to make."

Haines narrowed his eyes as he considered the request. It might be unwise to stonewall. He had been rash in his decision to secret the body away - he could see that now. Nevertheless, it was done. His newfound commanding persona served him well once again.

"This is a military investigation. If I need assistance I'll request it."

"The murderer could easily be a civilian."

"If so you'll be informed. I want that man Gunn. If you want to accomplish something find him. And send in my Ensign when you leave," Haines ordered.

The sheriff clenched his jaw and glared at the arrogant commander. Haines held his look, quite enjoying the virtual arm-wrestling. He learned more about power every moment. It could be snatched out of the ether at will and wielded like a weapon or dished out with largesse to inspire fealty.

"You are dismissed," he informed Stewart, and then kept his eyes on the man as he stomped from the room.

Haines turned back to his notes with a deep sigh of self-satisfaction. When the Ensign responded to the summons delivered by the sheriff, he reported that one Dr. Nicholas Denman and his young son were at the front desk asking about the promise the Admiral had made just before the ball the previous evening. The clerk at the front desk had attempted to weasel out of the offer made by the commanding officer, claiming that the Admiral was far too busy to approach with the subject and that it could set a potentially overwhelming precedent. The poor little fellow was down in the lobby now shedding very loud tears over the matter. Haines did not give it one second of consideration.

"Get rid of them," he commanded, "and then bring me the girl. I've waited long enough."

Chapter 17

At twenty-two Ensign Darrell Stroud was one of the youngest commissioned officers in the fleet. As the eldest of six children and the only boy, he had made it his mission to exceed the expectations of his family, lofty as they were, and at twenty graduated with distinction from the United States Naval Academy at Annapolis, then subsequently glided past most of his peers and out to sea. Ensign Stroud was a solid chunk of a man, square shouldered and broad chested, whose military haircut only served to enhance the squareness of his head and chiseled jaw.

Curiosity was not a characteristic encouraged or condoned along the chain of naval command. But he was curious – *it* was curious – the way Rear Admiral Haines was conducting the investigation into the killing of Captain John Adams. Ensign Stroud had felt no great respect for the deceased Captain. He found the man transparent in his manipulation of the men in his charge, and even of the officers above him, for his personal enhancement. The Captain's eye was so focused on the future that events unfolding around him were often ignored or worse, misunderstood. Ensign Stroud had been relieved when Rear Admiral Haines assumed command, appreciating the older man's adherence to military protocol and how the pomp and frivolity in the succession of seaports failed to impress him. Stroud had an uneasy feeling about the Admiral now however, and it was increasingly difficult to keep his curiosity at bay.

The thing was, Ensign Stroud was pretty sure he knew what happened, and because he knew he wondered at the Admiral's chosen course of action. Stroud occupied the room on the other side of Captain

Adams from Admiral Haines, located at the end of the interior corridor. He was in his room at the time of the unhappy event. He heard the sounds of the escalating argument between Captain Adams and a woman, and opened his door just a crack when the quarrel worsened to shouting and commotion in the hallway. He was in his skivvies though. He saw the Mongoloid child kicking and biting the Captain, then saw the Captain knock the boy away and was about to charge into the hallway himself when he saw Rear Admiral Haines had come out of his room. Thinking the Admiral would get the situation in hand he closed his door to finish dressing. Ensign Stroud was certain the kid had not intended to kill Captain Adams, but he was not certain why Haines was apparently protecting him. Was it for the mother? Was it some kind of grand gesture? Was it…what was it? And then Haines sent him to find those businessmen, and that pretty but useless girl that was always drooling around the Captain. What did they have to do with anything? He wondered if he should just tell Rear Admiral Haines what he had seen, but for some reason it gave him an uneasy feeling. He wanted someone else to know what he knew.

He worried these thoughts around in his mind as he rode the elevator to the main floor, resentful that his duties now included dealing with the tantrum of a disappointed child. It was easy to locate the object of his appointed task once he arrived in the lobby. There he saw Patrick, ever the young thespian, with arms folded across his chest, glowering and sniffling as his father hovered over him hoping for the promise of the visit to the ship to be made good. Remarkably, when Ensign Stroud delivered the bad news, that the trip was not to be, the boy seemed to recover immediately, and Stroud was clueless enough about children to notice that all the crying had not resulted in any actual tears.

He turned back to the elevator intending to execute his next distasteful order, delivering Lilly White to Rear Admiral Haines, when he saw that the doctor and his son were joined by the sheriff and that they fell into deep conversation while standing by one of the pillars at the entry. Without thinking, Ensign Stroud changed course and approached the trio. He did not know what he was going to say until he said it and he directed a question to Sheriff Stewart.

"Excuse me, Sir, may I have a word with you? And the doctor?"

Sheriff Stewart and Nicholas shared a look and then Nicholas instructed his son to stay put as the three men stepped a short distance away.

"When they examine the body, they will find signs of kicking and biting," Ensign Stroud said. "I saw that happening just before the Captain was killed."

Nicholas and Sheriff Stewart stared at the young officer in stunned silence. Ensign Stroud cleared his throat. "It was a retarded kid. They had a fight."

"Does Admiral Haines have this information?" the sheriff asked.

"He was there when it happened. He saw it, too."

"That's interesting."

Stroud was clearly extremely uncomfortable confiding in civilians, and small wonder. The very act of doing so could imply that he was questioning the actions of his superior officer – a fact not lost on the other two men.

Nicholas asked how the Captain had died.

"A blow to the throat. The kid grabbed one of those heavy ashtrays they have in all the rooms. It crushed his windpipe. I'm sure it was an accident."

"Did you see him do it?" the sheriff asked.

"No, Sir. I transported the body to the ship for autopsy."

"Do you think the Admiral saw it?"

"Unknown, Sir."

Nicholas and the sheriff made eye contact, each wondering what to do with this new revelation.

"You've done the right thing in telling us," Sheriff Stewart reassured the young officer.

"Yes, Sir," said Ensign Stroud, but he wasn't sure at all. He turned on his heel and made his way to the elevator simultaneously wracked with guilt yet slightly relieved for having shared the heavy burden of doubt and suspicion.

* * *

At seven o'clock the five would-be detectives gathered at a table in the Potter dining room. They had chosen a table slightly removed from the main bustle of activity and Nicholas ordered soup and bread for everyone as they sat down to hash over the new information each had collected. Nat Stewart began with the surprising disclosure by the young Ensign.

He asked, "But why would the Admiral keep it quiet? And why is he keeping me at arm's length? There's something else. Something we're not seeing."

"Quincy didn't do it," Patrick said with absolute certainty. The adults turned to give him their attention.

"I played with him that one time. He could kick and bite all right, but he wouldn't look for something to clobber him with. He doesn't think about things." He then added, "But if he was there so was his mom."

The others looked from one to another as the consequences of that reality sunk in.

Leontine said, "It could explain her reaction. There was something queer about it. But a murderer? I don't know."

"I don't really have a good feeling about Lilly White," Daisy confessed. "Sure, she was in love with the guy, but he was married and likely to stay that way. She was completely deranged - and accusing everyone she could think of."

"It wouldn't be the first love affair that ended with a body," Nicholas said. "And it's not hard to imagine her grabbing for the nearest weapon."

"What about the business of those two men? I sure would like to find the fellow from San Francisco," the sheriff added.

"Captain Adams was trying to help Magness in exchange for money," Daisy said. "I don't know why he would kill him before the plan was executed. And I've looked and looked and I can't find Kurt Gunn. Nobody can."

"Maybe I can," Stewart offered. "It's kind of the job. Does anyone know what he looks like?"

"I have a photo," Daisy told him.

"The Admiral was there, too. What about him?" Patrick asked.

The sheriff shook his head. "I don't mind saying I don't like him, but why would he do it? If he didn't want him around he could send him somewhere else. Besides, he's not the type. Trust me on that."

The group finished their light dinner and agreed to the next steps of their investigation and then went their separate ways.

Sheriff Stewart went to the front desk to secure the room number of

Kurt Gunn. Not surprisingly a knock at the man's door proved fruitless however. The hotel staff assured the sheriff they would notify the next shift of clerks and he would be contacted if the gentleman turned up. Stewart then asked for Steven Magness's room number and learned that Mr. Magness had checked out of the hotel not more than an hour ago, though his bag was still over by the porter's station. The desk clerk suggested that the sheriff might inquire in the lounge and Stewart acknowledged that checking in with the bartender was undoubtedly a good course of action in any case.

The bar was busy, locals and fleet officers packed like sardines and drinking plenty. It would be another hectic night for law enforcement. Daisy had supplied the sheriff with a description of Steven Magness and sitting at the bar, one foot on the ground as if ready to bolt, was his man. Working his way to stand next to him, Stewart made certain the businessman had a look at his badge as he leaned an elbow on the bar and looked him in the face.

"Steven Magness?"

Magness tilted his head back and threw the remainder of a drink down his throat, then locked eyes with the lawman.

"Can I help you with something?"

The question was slightly challenging.

"I hear you're leaving today. Where you headed?"

"San Diego."

"It might have to wait a day or two."

"That's not possible."

The sheriff pursed his lips, let out a breath and then stood up straight so that Magness had to look up at him.

"Check back into the hotel, Mr. Magness. Make it easy on us both."

Magness mulled over the implied threat. He motioned to the bartender for another drink. Why not? he thought to himself. He hadn't done anything - nothing this guy cared about. A couple of days wouldn't make any difference. He could run for Mexico any time.

"Sure," he finally replied, and then turned his back on the lawman and waited for his drink.

"I'm looking for a man name of Kurt Gunn," the sheriff said to the back of the other man's head.

"Never had the pleasure," Magness replied without turning around. The sheriff made an internal note of the obvious lie and then left the man to his drink. While he was at the hotel he decided he may as well get another look at the Rear Admiral in light of all the new information and he headed for the elevators.

At that particular moment, Lilly White was sitting across the desk from Admiral Haines. He thought she looked a mess. He was determined to learn from her the mechanics of the intrigue surrounding the report destined for her father.

"I'm well aware you met with Steven Magness in Los Angeles and that Captain Adams was somehow involved with the report about the railway deaths."

Lilly was shocked and her mind spun for a moment, reflexively searching for a story in defense of John Adams. It was only a few seconds though before reality stopped the automatic scheming in its tracks.

"None of that matters any more."

God, how she hated this man. If he wasn't such a pathetic little squirrel she could almost believe that he had killed John.

"It's not for you to decide what matters. I think the whole business got out of control and it cost him his life. Where is Kurt Gunn?"

"How would I know? Maybe he's at church praying for forgiveness for killing one of the finest men who ever lived."

Haines could see she was dangerously close to tears again. Women were so weak.

"What was Captain Adams' precise involvement with Magness?"

Lilly looked at the floor. What difference did it make? For all she cared everybody could know everything. None of it would bring John back.

"We were going to the newspapers. Steven Magness was paying John to discredit the report about the railway accidents before it got to my father. Kurt Gunn didn't know anything about it." How important it had all seemed just the day before.

"Where were you this morning between ten and eleven a.m.?"

"I don't know."

"You would do well to remember."

The interview over, Lilly wandered back to her room and rang room service. She would need strong spirits to get her through this night.

Only minutes after Lilly left the Rear Admiral, the sheriff tapped at his door. Haines was tired and had not sent for anyone further. He did not bother to disguise his annoyance.

"Who is it?"

"Nat Stewart," the sheriff called through the closed door.

"Who? What do you want? Come in." He glared at the lawman once he stepped into the room. "State your business, Sheriff. I'm on my way downstairs to eat."

"It just occurred to me, Admiral, that while you're getting statements from everyone at the hotel, someone should probably get a statement from you. You were in the next room when it happened, right?"

For the briefest of seconds Percifal Haines felt a crack in his veneer. To conceal the moment he slammed his hands on his desk and pushed himself to a forceful stand.

"Your orders were to deliver Kurt Gunn. Until you manage to complete that one task stop wasting my time."

Haines walked around his desk, jerked open the door and then stood there, an expectant look on his face, as he waited for the sheriff to leave.

Interesting. Stewart thought to himself as he left.

Chapter 18

The following morning Leontine and Patrick picked up Lindy Sue from the Tally Ho and made their way to Micheltorena Street. Patrick sat in front of Leontine in the saddle and as the horse plodded her way up Santa Barbara Street, Tesla tore out ahead of them, then circled back and darted in and out of Lindy Sue's legs. The horse tossed her head and snorted more in playfulness than annoyance and then Tesla would run around and bark at the mare and do it all again. Leontine found she liked the feeling of her arms encircling Patrick's slight body as she gently guided their path with the reins.

Once again, she was not entirely clear about what she hoped to achieve in further conversation with Elizabeth Adams. She resolved to keep her mind open and do nothing more than listen should Mrs. Adams find herself willing to share her thoughts. Patrick seemed more introspective than usual and Leontine offered herself as an audience for his reflections as well.

"I used to feel bad for Quincy when I first saw him," he admitted, "but now I think it's kind of good that he doesn't really know what happened."

"He probably does know in a way. I'm sure he can sense that something is terribly wrong."

"How could somebody just kill someone? They'd have to be crazy."

"It is hard to imagine, but people are sometimes driven to it. I suppose they think there is no other choice."

"We should just find the craziest person and that's probably the one who did it."

She didn't say so, but Leontine thought that was undoubtedly a good idea, though impossible to execute as craziness could be so effectively disguised.

In the end the trip proved fruitless. There was nobody home. Leontine left a note offering tea and company if Mrs. Adams wanted someone to talk with and then she and Patrick turned around and headed back downtown.

* * *

Elizabeth Adams and her son were at that moment seated across from Rear Admiral Haines in his interrogation room at the Potter. She had now had an entire day for the event to sink in and decided that the course initially chosen wanted correcting. It was her intention to encourage Rear Admiral Haines to admit to the deed. She would testify – if it came to that – that it had been an accident. He had come to her defense and the defense of her helpless child. She could think of no reason for him to object. Surely he would not want this frightening specter hanging over his head for the rest of his days. But she was wrong.

"It's too late for that," Haines said. His eyes narrowed with the heightened, desperate scrutiny of a hunted animal as he watched the woman's internal struggle play across her face.

"Why should I protect you?"

"It's the right thing to do."

"An innocent person will be accused."

"That doesn't have to happen. I'm in control of the investigation."

Elizabeth looked over at her son. Quincy sat quietly, staring vacantly into space, his jaw slack and his tongue visible between his teeth. She felt for a moment that she wanted to do what was right - for him. This was a well-defined example of right and wrong. Just and unjust. And then her heart broke as it did a hundred times a day as she realized there was nothing for Quincy in any of this. And yet…

"I can't do it. I won't. I have to tell what I know."

"I'll deny it – and name your son as the killer if you force my hand."

Elizabeth went silent and looked over once more at her boy.

"Mrs. Adams, you can't think that your unfortunate son – however fond of him you are – is as important as an Admiral in the United States naval command."

Quincy seemed to sense his mother's gaze and his face lit up, beaming and completely joyous in her attention and she knew instantly, that was exactly what she thought.

"I'll consider what you have said," she lied, and then gathered her son and left.

Percifal Haines did not have a good feeling about this.

* * *

Kurt Gunn regained consciousness with no idea where he was, what had been happening to him or for how long. His head was splitting and he had a foul taste in his mouth. It was all he could to do open his eyes a slit and when he did he had no frame of reference for what he saw. He closed his eyes again with a moan. A petite and very naked Chinese girl sleeping next to him stirred and sat up. Not bothering to cover herself, she rose from the bed and retrieved an opium pipe from the night table and then headed out to the kitchen to refill it – another workday begun.

When she returned to the room it was to find Gunn sitting up in bed, his head in his hands. She did not speak English and so was unable to answer the question he managed to voice.

"Where am I?" he croaked.

The teenaged prostitute held out the pipe. She had learned it was the answer for every question anyway. When the man declined she shrugged, put the thing in her mouth, struck a match and drew on it herself. Gunn lifted the bedcovers to see what he was wearing. Only his knee-length undergarment. He glanced over at the Chinese girl. She was a child really, now perched on the edge of the bed staring sightlessly out the window, still completely naked. Gunn raked his fingers through his wiry gray hair and whiskers. He squinted at the sparse gray hairs on his chest and the expansive melon of his belly and then again at the girl. He wished she would put something on. Or leave the room. He needed to try to stand up and was embarrassed by his state of undress. He closed his eyes and tried to remember whatever unseemly actions he had engaged in with the young girl, but thankfully could remember nothing. Finally he cleared his throat to gain her attention and then motioned toward the door to communicate that he wanted some privacy. She seemed to immediately understand. She stood and retrieved a threadbare yet vibrantly colored silk wrap lying in a heap on the floor, slipped into it and disappeared from the room. Gunn threw back the covers and struggled to his feet. He had never experienced a headache so blinding and painful but needed to look out the window to try to learn where he was. He parted the heavy tapestry draperies and squinted at the street outside but of course it was meaningless. This was not his city. He closed his eyes against the pain of the light. Feeling nauseous, he turned to grope his way back to the bed but didn't make it and collapsed unconscious on the floor.

* * *

Leontine, Patrick and Lindy Sue clopped down State Street to Nicholas Denman's office. She planned to drop Patrick off and then hurry back to the Birabent Market to help Uncle Remi. The store had been extremely busy because of all the activity downtown and her poor uncle was doing more than his share while she chased around trying to help solve a murder. Patrick had just jumped off the horse when his father joined them out on the sidewalk.

"Kurt Gunn was brought to St. Francis Hospital half an hour ago," he related with some excitement.

"What happened to him?" Patrick asked.

"I don't know yet. Dr. Morrey saw him. As soon as I saw his name in the register I came back to town. We need to find the sheriff."

"Who delivered him to the hospital?" Leontine asked.

"I don't know."

"Will he be there long enough?"

"I asked the nurse to make sure he stayed put for a while. And I hid his clothes," Nicholas admitted with a somewhat sheepish grin.

Leontine said, "Maybe Daisy can leave work for a bit. The more of us searching, the better."

Nicholas agreed to wait at his office to be by a telephone so those looking would have a central place to report. He had patients to see in any case. Leontine thought for the first time what a convenience it would be to have a telephone of her own. They had seemed frivolous to her until recently and now she felt the need of one at every turn. However enjoyable the futile visit to Mrs. Adams' home just completed had been, it was a fine example of effort that could have been spared through use of telephone communication. They decided Patrick would lead Lindy Sue back to the Tally Ho and search both sides of State Street for Sheriff Stewart on the way while Leontine headed for City Hall Plaza to see if she could spring Daisy to aid in the search.

Once arrived, Leontine entered the interior of the *Daily News* production room and immediately spotted Daisy standing at one of the typesetting tables situated along one wall. The opposing wall was lined with desks, each one a haphazard collection of a typewriter, note books, loose papers and fountain pens. There were no people at the desks at the moment, as no doubt they were wandering the city in search of events to write about. If they only knew. The center of the room was dominated by the printing press, its industrial smells and mysterious parts fascinating even in stillness. The thing was as big as a carriage and two men were tending to it while the newspaper manager, Clarence Miller, monitored their efforts through the window of his enclosed office at the far end of the room. He furrowed his brow in obvious displeasure as he watched Leontine approach his worker.

Leontine hurriedly filled her friend in on the latest development, not wanting to cause trouble for her at work. Daisy instructed Leontine to give her five minutes and she would join her outside. As she left Leontine nodded to Mr. Miller and winced at Daisy when he did not respond, then scurried outside. Daisy took a breath, lifted her chin and approached her boss, leaning into his office.

"A word?" she asked. Miller motioned Daisy to a chair across from his desk but she chose to remain standing.

"There's a huge story about to break open and I need a little time away this morning to try to get to the bottom of it. None of the other papers have any idea. It'll be quite a scoop."

"What story?"

"I can't say yet. I need time."

Miller furrowed his brow, his head already shaking 'no' before he said a word. Daisy pursed her lips, frustrated, as she waited for what was sure to be an overwrought reply. He could be such a windbag. Clarence Miller thought and thought and then:

"I wonder Miss Merrie, if you had occasion to hire a man to repair your front step and when he showed up he proposed to fix your roof instead, what it is you think you would do?"

When Daisy did not immediately respond, he continued, "Let us say further that your roof was actually in good shape – in no need of repair, as it were. How would you respond to his request in that event?"

"More to the point, Mr. Miller," Daisy asked, "what would you do?"

"I'm afraid I'd have to let him go."

He felt certain his allegory would hit home and Daisy would respond to the warning and return to the typesetting table. To his surprise and exasperation Daisy broke into a grin. She thrust an arm over his desk to extract a handshake.

"Great! Thanks for the start, Mr. Miller!" Then she bolted from the room.

Clarence Miller sat in stunned silence not knowing for certain if he still had a typesetter for the day.

* * *

Once out on the street the women split up. They had a pretty good idea of the places Sheriff Stewart would be looking for Kurt Gunn so they decided the best course of action was for Daisy to take the trolley to the Potter to look for him there while Leontine scoured the lower blocks of State Street that Patrick would not pass by on his way to the Tally Ho.

It was Leontine who found their man outside the Gutierrez Drug Store. He was walking against the crowd, eyes probing every face. He was so intent in observing the men he did not immediately notice Leontine standing right in front of him.

"Kurt Gunn has surfaced," she told him, a bit surprised at her own level of excitement. "We're all looking for you. I need to report you've been found."

Leontine went inside the drug store to use their telephone to call Nicholas who in turn phoned the Potter and left a message for Daisy that they had located the sheriff and they would all meet her at the hotel once they learned what, if any, light Kurt Gunn could shed on anything.

Nat Stewart's horse was tethered at his office in City Hall Plaza and he hurried in that direction as Leontine made her way to the Tally Ho to retrieve Patrick and see if they could hang onto Lindy Sue a bit longer.

They would connect at St. Francis Hospital as soon as the horses could get them there.

With Patrick once again sharing the saddle, the two headed north on State Street north toward Micheltorena Street on which they would travel east to the outskirts of town where the hospital was located. The city was expanding so quickly it seemed and there were clusters of homes even north of Mission Street now and several on Grand Avenue with spectacular views overlooking the city and the Channel Islands beyond.

The gathering activity of the day was generating a steadily increasing stream of sailors and reveling locals moving like a trail of ants between Stearns Wharf all the way up State Street to the Arlington Hotel. One had to wonder how the city would have coped with the fleet prior to the completion of the expansive Potter Hotel. Though the Arlington was grand by any standard and included many additional rooms in the Arlington Annex on Victoria Street, it would have proved inadequate in the extreme for the events at hand, to say nothing of the distance from the shore. It was definitely worth the trek from the hub of activities downtown however, to enjoy the sprawling views of the ocean, the city and the old Mission visible from the porch and viewing decks at the Arlington.

It was fully an hour before the four finally met up at St. Francis Hospital. Nicholas asked Patrick to wait outside Kurt Gunn's room. He had interviewed enough patients in his practice to know there were plenty of topics he would wish to shield Patrick from at his young age.

The boy was clearly crestfallen, though he did not argue. Leontine bit her tongue at first. She knew if Daisy were there she would have lobbied for Patrick's inclusion. She felt Patrick's eyes on her, silently pleading for her to come to his aid. In the end she decided to try on a little of her tenant's boldness to see how it would feel.

"I understand your urge to protect your son, Dr. Denman," she said, "though I can't help but wonder what could be more disturbing than the murder itself. His insights are so valuable, I wonder if you might reconsider."

Nicholas tried to keep irritation from showing on his face. He was beginning to feel undermined by Leontine's repeated intrusions and was growing weary of the feeling that he was somehow in competition with her for his son's affection. A competition he felt he was losing. He did not know it, but all of his misgivings were clearly telegraphed by his expression. Leontine immediately regretted her foray into assertiveness and backtracked as quickly as she could.

"I see I've overstepped," she said. "I apologize. I'll wait out here with Patrick. I'm sure you and the sheriff are more than capable of extracting any useful information from Mr. Gunn."

Nicholas ran his hand through his hair. This was worse. Not only did it seem his fault that the two of them were excluded, he and the sheriff would also be deprived of their combined points of view. He swallowed his pride if not his annoyance.

"No, come in. Both of you."

Nicholas opened the door to Kurt Gunn's room. There were four beds in the room, two on each side, each supplied with a curtain to provide at least some small measure of discretion. Gunn sat on the edge of the bed closest to the door. The curtain was drawn around the bed in the opposing corner, no doubt shielding some unfortunate within, and the other two beds were empty at the moment. Gunn wore his undergarments covered by a rough cotton shift supplied by the hospital. He looked up at the group entering his room but his expression showed no curiosity. He immediately lowered his head. Dr. Denman and Sheriff Stewart approached the bedside, Leontine and Patrick hanging back by the door.

"It smells in here," Patrick whispered to his friend, his face scrunched against unpleasant and unfamiliar odors. She could only agree.

"How are you feeling?" Nicholas asked Gunn.

Gunn spoke without looking up. "My head is splitting and I feel sick to my stomach."

Nicholas picked up the medical chart from the bedside table.

"Opium dependence is a cruel taskmaster, Mr. Gunn. How long have you been using it?"

"I don't know. What day is this?"

"It's Tuesday, the twenty-eighth of April," Dr. Denman said. "Mr. Gunn, the sheriff is here and would like to ask some questions. Do you feel well enough to answer?"

Kurt Gunn finally looked up and registered a moment of interest at the four people standing in his room. He shrugged in response to the question, sat on his hands and looked down at his lap.

"Mr. Gunn, Captain John Adams has been found murdered in his room at the Potter Hotel," the sheriff said.

That got Gunn's attention.

"Did I do it?" he asked, seemingly resigned to an answer in the affirmative.

"I don't know. Where were you yesterday morning between ten and eleven?"

"I can't remember. I don't know what happened. I checked in to my room and then I was going to have a look around the hotel. The next thing I knew I woke up at…." Gunn trailed off casting a sidelong glance at the woman and child standing by the door. It seemed inappropriate to mention the brothel in their presence.

At this point Leontine could see that she and Patrick were having an adverse effect on the questioning. She looked over at Nicholas, intending to acknowledge the correctness of his initial instinct, but he was absorbed in his patient and though he heard the two exit the room he did not remove his attention from Kurt Gunn.

"I'm going to prescribe you some Bayer Aspirin, Mr. Gunn. And I'm instructing the nurse to administer 48 ounces of Veronica Springs Medicinal Water. It will ease another unfortunate side effect. You'll feel better this afternoon."

The sheriff said, "Go back to the hotel, Mr. Gunn. There will be more questions later."

"I'll try my best to answer them," Gunn replied. "Has anyone seen my pants?"

The four gathered in the hallway after the interview. Nicholas said he needed to return to work. The others agreed to make their way to the Potter Hotel to reconnect with Daisy and decide on the next course of action once Leontine and Patrick returned Lindy Sue to the Tally Ho and the sheriff stopped at his office to make sure no worse calamity had befallen the city that morning.

It was over an hour later that Leontine, Patrick and the sheriff arrived once again at the Potter by trolley. They easily located Daisy on the sun porch in conversation with Lilly White and her Aunt Anne. Patrick was eager to fill Daisy in on the visit with Kurt Gunn but paused before speaking, not certain about the presence of the other two women.

At that moment Steven Magness arrived on the deck, drink in hand. He acknowledged Daisy and then the sheriff with a nod and moved to the railing as if to take in the view, but they were all well aware that he was close enough to overhear anything they might say. No matter who was in attendance, Patrick could wait no longer to tell Daisy the news.

"We all saw Kurt Gunn," burst out of him. His eyes swept the attendant adults to make sure it was okay to divulge the information in their current setting – now that he had already done so.

It was fortuitous that Leontine's resting gaze included both Steven Magness and Lilly White in her field of view. At the mention of Kurt Gunn, the glance that passed between them did so in the blink of an eye. Leontine's first instinct was to keep the observation to herself so that she could consider its meaning and then bring it forward later if necessary for the amateur detectives to ruminate over as a group. However, she quickly realized she would then have to fill in each of the other investigators separately, and here they all were, so she addressed her suspicion immediately.

Leontine said, "Miss White, I wonder if you have known of the whereabouts of Mr. Gunn all along."

The others, surprised at her accusation, turned their attention to the girl for her response.

"Of course not," Lilly insisted, eyelashes fluttering feverishly. "I had no idea where he was."

But a second split-second glance at Magness gave her away. Sheriff Stewart made sense of the exchange immediately.

"Join us Mr. Magness," he said to the man. Magness turned to face the group fully but did not move any closer. Lilly looked to her Aunt for support, but Anne was watching her niece with the same expression as the others, distrust. Lilly let her head fall back and she closed her eyes. There was no point in being secretive she decided once again. She wanted John's murderer found out and if these people could uncover who had committed the crime then she was determined to give them what they needed.

"It was part of John's plan to discredit Gunn's report," she admitted, "but I didn't know where he was. Exactly."

Magness turned away and looked out to the Pacific Ocean. Mexico was calling. He could be gone by sunset. For several moments the entire group was silent, each lost in their own contemplation, trying to connect dots that were too disparate to form a cohesive picture.

Sheriff Stewart rubbed the back of his neck while he tried to come up with some kind of a plan. Normally he would detain Magness and probably even Lilly White in order to thoroughly and properly question them about every aspect of their association with the deceased Captain and each other, but that was simply impossible. The population of the city had more than doubled overnight if you counted the sailors still out in the channel waiting their turn to come ashore. The correct thing to do was report his suspicions to Rear Admiral Haines so that he could confine and question these two so obviously up to their necks in whatever dark business had resulted in the death of the Captain, but the Rear Admiral himself was technically on their list of suspects and, though he did not personally seriously believe Haines was their man, he couldn't reconcile how to bring him inside the circle of information gathering and keep him on the outside at the same time. In the end all he could do was basically make a request and do his best to present is as an order.

"Miss White, I'm afraid I must confine you to the hotel until these claims can be examined. That goes for you, too, Mr. Magness."

Magness turned his back on the group without voicing his acceptance.

"I'll do as you ask, of course," Lilly said. "I want nothing more than for the murderer to be brought to justice." She dabbed at delicate tears collecting in the corner of one eye.

The hostess and her chaperone retired from the deck and Leontine, Patrick, Daisy and the sheriff put their heads together to identify the next logical steps.

The sheriff said, "I need to take care of some things in town, but I suggest we meet again here in the dining room at 7:00. We're going to make sense of this thing once and for all."

Daisy decided it would help her to write down the jumble of facts as they currently understood them. She processed information better when writing and she promised to share her report when they reconnected.

Leontine needed to get back to the store and asked Patrick if he would like to join her. She suspected Uncle Remi could use his help stocking and organizing shelves and besides, she didn't want him to be alone after all this disturbing activity.

When they got back to the Birabent Market it was to find Elizabeth Adams and Quincy waiting patiently for them inside. Remi assured his niece that he had matters well in hand. He did like the idea of Patrick giving him some help and even thought they could find something to occupy Quincy. Leontine and Elizabeth retreated upstairs.

This time Elizabeth sat at Leontine's kitchen table. She waited quietly while Leontine prepared tea, watching her movements, thoughts suspended for the moment. When Leontine sat across from her at the table however, Elizabeth worried about what she would say. The truth was, she liked Leontine. There were few enough people she felt comfortable around and as a result she was, for the most part, a stranger to intimate conversation. She didn't know where to begin.

For her part, Leontine had a sense that the Captain's wife was in search of a confidante. Something was troubling her terribly, aside from the obvious, the loss of her husband. Leontine acknowledged to herself that if she wanted the other woman to be truthful with her she should well start with some truths of her own.

Leontine said, "I need to correct a misconception that I should not have let stand so long. Patrick is not my son, though it would delight me if that were the case. His mother died when he was barely more than a baby. We have become close friends."

"I thought you seemed young to have a child his age."

"I wonder how you are faring, Mrs. Adams. I find I worry about you. Here you have suffered this terrible loss and your life requires that you carry on almost as if it had never happened."

Elizabeth Adams sighed deeply, her gaze fixed sightlessly inward.

"Thank you, Miss Birabent. Truly. But my world is so small. What does it matter, really, if I'm happy or sad? There is no one to notice."

"Each of us feels joy and pain, Mrs. Adams, no doubt in equal measure. Only the very calloused are not moved to share in another's happiness, or ease their discomfort if they can. In that way your sorrow matters to us all."

The young widow tightened her lips to stop the lower one from quivering, dangerously close to letting loose a long overdue accumulation of tears.

"I feel I should tell you that I know you quarreled with your husband just prior to his death and that Quincy reacted badly and attacked his father. A young Ensign was in the next room and saw the altercation in the hallway."

Elizabeth Adams looked into Leontine's eyes as she tried to decide what to say. She wanted to admit everything, but she was afraid. Afraid of what Admiral Haines might do. Afraid she could lose her son.

"I want you to know that I do not believe Quincy killed his father," Leontine continued, "But I also believe you might know who did. I'm not asking you to tell me. I only want you to consider your own well-being. Please know I will support you any way I can."

"Thank you," Elizabeth murmured, and at last the tears escaped.

Chapter 19

Early that evening, Percifal Haines made the decision to eat in the dining room. He had spent the entire day interviewing hotel staff and those occupying nearby rooms and now felt certain that no one had seen or heard anything that put him in a compromising light. He instructed his Ensign to make the necessary arrangements and in a fit of magnanimity invited the young officer to join him. He did not sense the man's hesitation. It would never occur to him.

Once in the dining room the Rear Admiral's mood improved even more. The place was impressive and agreeable in every way and those in the fleet lucky enough to be there were obviously enjoying the time of their lives. He felt moved by his own benevolence, a generous and caring patriarch, and he smiled as he looked around the room. He had never engaged Ensign Stroud in conversation and so did not know that he was uncharacteristically subdued. He was surprised therefore, when the young officer confessed to him that he had something of grave import on his mind.

As Ensign Stroud related what he had seen in the corridor just prior to the murder, the Rear Admiral kept his eyes on his subordinate as his mind began crafting an unassailable response that it had ready to deliver before the younger man even finished his tale. Yes, he had followed into Captain Adams' room with the troubled family. The mother had been able to soothe the retarded boy and they apologized profusely for the disruption. When Admiral Haines left them, he explained, they assured him that they would resolve their family dispute at a lower volume. The Rear Admiral did not know how much longer the mother and unfortunate child remained in the room. The Captain's body had not been found until more than an hour later, which was more than enough time for nearly anyone to have entered the room and taken his life. Naturally, as a precaution, he told Ensign Stroud, he had spoken with the widow just this morning and had no reason to disbelieve her account that she and her son departed only minutes after he, himself, left the room. Haines was quite pleased with the narrative and felt certain he was able to ease the Ensign's mind while keeping options open to name whomever he ultimately chose to take the fall.

In truth, Ensign Stroud was not so sure. He had seen the ashtray in the Admiral's hand when he burst into the hallway. He wanted to ask how the retarded kid had ended up with it. He nearly brought it up but something gave him pause. It sounded like an accusation. As the Admiral spoke, the young man's mind worried at the excluded detail and as a consequence he only half registered his commanding officer's explanation.

As the two officers conversed, Leontine, Patrick, Nicholas, Daisy and Sheriff Stewart met at what was becoming their customary table, discussing new developments once again over soup and bread. Daisy began by pulling out the several sheets of notes she had created that afternoon. A fresh page listed the names of the principal characters and she proposed that they now discuss each one with an eye toward crossing them off the list of suspects. The first name was Lilly White.

"Her sorrow seems genuine to me," Leontine offered by way of beginning the evaluation.

"Maybe," said Sheriff Stewart, "but she is also a liar."

"Lying and withholding information are not exactly the same," Daisy protested. "She loved him and tries to protect him even now."

"One could argue that hopeless love for a married man makes her more of a suspect than less of one," Nicholas pointed out.

Daisy replied, "It's hard to imagine a scenario that would end with her grabbing an ashtray and doing him in. She might be capable of such violence if under attack, but we know it was Quincy who did the kicking and biting. I can't picture her ending a lover's quarrel that way."

"I'm nearly convinced Elizabeth Adams knows who is responsible," Leontine added. "If that is the case, and Lilly White the killer, why would she protect her husband's mistress?"

They all looked from one to another to see if there was more to say. After a few moments Daisy took up her pen and drew a line through Lilly's name. Next on the list was Kurt Gunn.

"He seems more convinced of his own guilt than anyone," Nicholas said. "It's almost as if he would welcome the punishment."

Daisy added, "It's true his motive is the most clear because of Adams' threat to his character."

"His alibi is easy enough to check out," Sheriff Stewart said. "I'll pay a visit to Ling Fan."

The next name on the list was Quincy, followed by that of his mother. The others turned to Leontine, knowing she was in a position to understand most about the unlucky pair.

She said, "My heart tells me neither one is responsible, but I'm not sure I have valid reasons to cross either of them off the list."

Daisy sat back. Only one name - Lilly White - had been crossed off.

"You forgot Admiral Haines," Patrick reminded Daisy.

"We never came up with a reason for him to do it," said the sheriff.

"Maybe he has one and we just never thought of it," Patrick replied with a shrug.

Leontine asked, "Why do you think we should consider him?"

Patrick stared at his soup, filling and emptying his spoon as he thought it over. "I don't know," he said, finally. "He reminds me of Billy Kilgore, I guess."

That earned a raised eyebrow from both Leontine and Daisy. They had seen Billy Kilgore after all, and knew him to be a terrible bully. Is that what Patrick sensed? But a bully is hardly a murderer. Nevertheless, Daisy met the eye the others at the table each in turn and, receiving no objection, added Rear Admiral Haines' name to the bottom of the list.

No sooner had Daisy finished writing his name, than the man himself approached their table, trailed by an extremely pensive Ensign Stroud. It was challenging for each of them to maintain expressions of casual innocence as the man truly in charge of the murder investigation appeared. Leontine marveled at him as the Admiral stood across from her. Could this be the same ineffectual commander she had seen just two nights previously? The officer before her seemed robust in comparison. The Admiral registered no hint of recognition for either Leontine or Patrick. In fact, he quite ignored everyone at the table with the exception of the sheriff.

"I'd like a word with you," he said, and moved a few feet away, assuming his order would be obeyed. He therefore did not see the reassuring glance directed at his subordinate officer, the other men communicating that their earlier conversation would remain secret.

"The investigation is proceeding well. I will have all I need in advance of departure on Thursday."

Sheriff Stewart sized the man up for a moment. In light of the conversation he had been involved in not thirty seconds earlier, he suddenly felt reluctant to supply him with information. However, the Rear Admiral was technically in charge and had a right to know about the appearance of the chagrined Kurt Gunn and his stint at Ling Fan's establishment. He reluctantly informed the Admiral about the morning's activities.

"A *Chinese* whore house?" Haines repeated in disbelief. The very idea was completely repugnant him on so many levels.

"It was apparently Captain Adams' idea -- to make him look bad."

"Indeed. And where will I find Mr. Gunn now?"

"He's probably back here at the hotel by now."

"I'll see him in the morning. Is there anything else?"

"Not unless you have anything."

Admiral Haines looked over to Ensign Stroud and jerked his head in the direction of the elevators indicating their departure and then turned and walked away. No "thank you", no parting comment. Not even a salute. Sheriff Stewart returned to the table and sat down to his soup with a sigh.

"I do not like that man," he admitted as he picked up his spoon.

* * *

Later that night Ensign Stroud found himself walking up Anacapa Street carrying a missive penned by his commanding officer to be delivered to the owner of an unsavory institution at the southeast corner of Anacapa and Canon Perdido Streets. Thankfully he did not have to actually pronounce the names of the streets as he passed by them and he wondered, not for the first time, what the residents of this seaside village had against the alphabet, trees or names of former presidents as markers to find their way as they wandered around town.

He was increasingly uneasy about the duties assigned to him by Rear Admiral Haines. He had been required to rouse Kurt Gunn from his bed and deliver him to the Rear Admiral's office shortly after returning to their rooms from the dining hall. He could not stop himself from questioning the command in his mind, having clearly heard the Admiral tell Sheriff Stewart he would talk to Gunn in the morning. Waking the businessman proved to be no easy task. It had been impossible to wake him from the hallway and he ended up enlisting the aid of the housekeeping staff to let him inside the room to physically shake Kurt Gunn awake. After a fairly brief conversation between Rear Admiral Haines and Mr. Gunn, Stroud was dispatched on his current undertaking; to deliver the note, with the added instruction to bring the owner of the brothel back to his commander once he had read it.

Ensign Stroud had never been inside a brothel before. From the outside it looked like a normal house, and a pleasant one at that. Across Canon Perdido Street he saw the grounds of the old Presidio and farther east along Canon Perdido street unmistakable indicators that this was the tiny city's version of Chinatown. He approached what he assumed was the main entrance as it was slightly larger than several other doors that could be entered from the wrap-around porch. He tried not to think what might be transpiring behind any one of them at this evening hour as he trudged up the half-dozen wooden steps. And then Ensign Stroud was, for a moment, at a loss. Did one knock or ring the bell or just open the door and walk in? Mostly because he was intimidated by what he might find upon entering, he arrived at the decision to knock.

It was several minutes before a surprisingly ordinary looking young Chinese girl opened the door wearing a modest, high-necked tunic over a long dark colored skirt. She bowed low and then stood aside and allowed him to pass inside. The interior was dimly lit, but as he stood in the entry hall he could make out comfortable cushioned furniture and red painted walls adorned with Asian art in what appeared to be the living room just off the entry. More art pieces and beautifully framed Chinese letters that looked more like art than words lined the long corridor of a hallway leading to the back of the house as well. The scent of the place was completely foreign to Stroud and he couldn't decide if it was pleasant or not. The muffled sounds of some kind of stringed instrument floated toward the entryway from somewhere inside.

The girl motioned for Ensign Stroud to enter and take a seat in the cozy space of the living room. He had no intention of making himself comfortable, however. As soon as the Ensign began speaking the Chinese girl bowed deeply and held the pose while he spoke which he found very unsettling.

"Is your boss here?" he asked.

The girl answered softly in Chinese, technically directing her answer to the floor.

"I don't understand you," he said, then continued more slowly and a little louder." I need to speak with whoever is in charge."

The girl motioned him into the living room with heightened enthusiasm and spoke once again in Chinese. Ensign Stroud looked into the room but feared going in there would create the wrong impression. He pulled the note from the pocket of his jacket and held it out to the girl.

"Give this to the owner, and I hope that's not you." He continued to press it in her direction until she had little choice but to take it.

With a final bow, the young girl turned and glided down the hallway in a graceful, swaying gait. Ensign Stroud replaced his cap, shoved his hands into his pockets and waited.

Minutes later he looked up to see a different woman coming in his direction. She wore men's dungarees and a man's cotton shirt and though at first she looked as young as the girl who had answered the door, her face seemed to age magically the closer she came. She held the opened note in one hand and a lit cigar in the other. When she stood in front of the Ensign – a little closer than he would have liked - she smiled, her teeth a ghastly yellow. No doubt she had the cigars to thank for that. Her English was broken but thankfully, discernible.

"I come for half hour. No more," she said, emphasizing the time limit with a judo chop to the air. "No inside. Outside kitchen. Ten o'clock. Half hour!" She then turned and strode back down the hallway.

* * *

When Nat Stewart arrived at the county courthouse building on Figueroa Street the following morning, he found Ling Fan, cigar in hand, sitting on the steps outside his office. They nodded to each other in greeting and the Chinese woman stood a little too close behind him puffing on her cigar as he fumbled with the keys. Once inside the sheriff circled around to his desk chair and took a seat. Ling Fan stayed right behind him standing just inches away when she began to speak.

"You got trouble with big ship man," she told him.

That was hardly news.

"He pay good money Ling Fan for lies to you."

That got the sheriff's attention. "Which ship man? What lies?"

Ling Fan placed her hand in the air just slightly over her own head indicating the stature of a short man, then put her thumbs in her armpits and puffed out her chest and marched around like a strutting rooster.

"That's gotta be Haines," Stewart said. "What lies?"

"One man pay, bring fat gray-hair man my house. Other man pay, say gray-hair man not my house. Me? Get pay, get pay. Fine. You got trouble."

"Why tell me if he paid you off?"

"Nat Stewart owe Ling Fan one. Ship sail away – no problem," and she showed him her yellow grin.

As soon as Ling Fan left his office, Sheriff Stewart locked up again and headed over to the Birabent Market. There was only one reason he could think of for Rear Admiral Haines to mess with Kurt Gunn's alibi. Whatever his motive, it looked a lot like Haines may have done the Captain in. The doctor's kid had it right after all.

Believing something and being able to prove it were two different things however. He remembered Leontine saying she thought Captain Adams' widow knew who had murdered her husband. If so, they needed to get her to admit who it was. Once the sheriff filled Leontine in on Haines' bribery intended to implicate Kurt Gunn, the two of them secured horses and rode side by side to the house on Micheltorena Street. They dismounted and tied the horses to the branches of a shrub near the street on the Adams property. The horses could easily pull the thing out of the ground if they really cared to escape, but fortunately were unaware of the fact.

When Elizabeth Adams responded to their knock at her door she seemed wary but really had no choice other than to invite them in. Once inside the widow's living room, the sheriff left it to Leontine to guide the conversation.

She said, "Mrs. Adams, we have reason to believe that Admiral Haines is attempting to implicate Kurt Gunn in the murder of Captain Adams."

"Kurt Gunn?" Elizabeth seemed confused by the report. Her expression clouded and her brow furrowed in thought. "This came from Admiral Haines? Are you certain?"

As gently as possible, Leontine said, "Mrs. Adams, forgive me, but if you know who is responsible for your husband's murder, it is now imperative that you reveal who it is."

Elizabeth Adams looked uncertain, her gaze shifting from Leontine to the sheriff and back.

"Did the killer threaten you in some way?" Leontine asked.

Elizabeth Adams covered her face with her hands and sunk onto a chair, unable hold back tears.

"He said he would name Quincy. I should have told someone immediately. Kurt Gunn did not do it. He is not the one."

Leontine pushed for an answer. "Will you tell us who it was?"

Elizabeth Adams looked into the eyes of her new friend. "It was Admiral Haines. He didn't mean to kill him, I'm sure of it. He just kind of went crazy. I told him I would swear it was an accident, but then he said it was too late and he would say Quincy did it and nobody would believe me and not him."

The sheriff said, "We believe you, Mrs. Adams. Will you testify to this?"

The young widow sighed and swiped at her tears, relieved beyond words to have the truth spoken at last.

"Yes, I will."

* * *

Not more than an hour later Sheriff Stewart knocked on Rear Admiral Haines' door on the fifth floor of the Potter Hotel and then stepped inside before Haines shouted the command to enter. He found the Admiral seated at his desk transferring papers and supplies to a box that would transport them out to the ship. He looked up from his work with some annoyance.

"I didn't send for you," he said.

"I checked out Kurt Gunn's alibi this morning," the sheriff told him. The Rear Admiral ceased his activity and leaned back in his chair.

"And what did you learn?"

"Santa Barbara is a small town, Admiral. I don't think you know what that means for people. People who will spend their entire lives together."

"Is there some reason I should care what it means?"

"You don't have to care, but it's too bad you didn't know."

Rear Admiral Haines blinked, the meaning behind the sheriff's words beginning to sink in.

"What exactly did the whore tell you?"

"She's not a whore, actually, just a very shrewd businesswoman."

"Whatever you think you know Sheriff, I assure you, where Kurt Gunn was or was not on Saturday morning is of little consequence."

The sheriff knew he shouldn't be enjoying this, but he couldn't quite help himself.

"If that's true, I have to ask myself why you would go to all the trouble to bribe Ling Fan to lie about where he was. It looked a little suspicious to me. And then who should show up but a perfectly good witness to the murder who is now willing to testify."

"She's protecting her idiot son, surely you can see that. My Ensign will swear he saw the boy attack his father. There is evidence of it on the victim's body."

"I didn't say the witness was Captain Adams' wife, but it doesn't surprise me you know who I meant. Not that it matters. Either act on its own might not make enough of a case, but when you add the two together -- a witness and the bribe, well. . . ." Sheriff Stewart gave a little shrug. "And you won't want lean too heavy on your Ensign. He's guarding the door now until the Naval Military Police arrive. You were right, it's a military matter after all."

When Sheriff Stewart left the room, Rear Admiral Haines was leaning back in his chair with his eyes closed looking very, very small.

* * *

In the dining room below Leontine, Patrick, Daisy and Nicholas were waiting for the sheriff to join them. Nicholas acknowledged that it was really too early for dinner, but then ordered soup anyway and some chocolate cake to celebrate. Nat Stewart arrived at the same time as the food.

"I pitched the story to the *Daily Independent*," Daisy told her friends. "The editor, Tom O'Brien, told me to write it up and if it's good enough we'll see where it goes. I told him he might as well just give me a job because it will definitely be good enough." The others heartily expressed their lack of doubt that she would be hired.

She added, "Lilly White has agreed to deliver the corporate documents to her father. I think she wants to try to make it up to Kurt Gunn."

"I imagine Magness lit out as soon as he was out of our sight," Sheriff Stewart surmised. "Let's hope the senator can pull enough strings to rein him back in."

The others agreed.

"This has been the best week of my whole life," Patrick gushed. "I hope something else bad happens so I can figure it out with Miss Birabent and Daisy."

As Nicholas protested that something bad need not happen and that there were plenty of pleasant things in the world that needed figuring out, Leontine leaned over to whisper in Patrick's ear:

"I think you should call me Lulubelle."

Annie J. Dahlgren

Annie has completed over a dozen screenplays, winning recognition on numerous occasions as quarter- or semi-finalist in such prestigious writing competitions as the Nicholl Fellowship, the Chesterfield Writing Fellowship, the Austin Film Festival competition and the LA Expo, among others.

In 2007 Annie co-wrote and co-produced a musical comedy for the stage, *Moment of Truth*, that was performed at the Center Stage Theater in Santa Barbara in June and July of that year. An earlier musical, *Fortunes Made*, was released as a music CD in 2005 and later as a narrated audio performance. In addition she has released four CDs of original music as a singer/songwriter. Her fifth CD is in process.

Annie is also a partner in Over 40 Productions, producing, directing and editing music videos for independently produced musicians in the Santa Barbara area.

2013 saw the production and release of her story *The Bet* by the "Community Film Studio Santa Barbara", a non-profit community-based production company of which she was a founding board member. The film took first prize at the La Femme Film Festival in Los Angeles and will soon be available in digital distribution.

Now beginning a new phase with the novel *A Murder at the Potter Hotel* in partnership with long-time local historian Neal Graffy, it is the first in a series of stories that will follow Leontine, Patrick and Daisy through the early years of 20th century Santa Barbara, California.

OTHER PROJECTS by Annie J. Dahlgren

Music CDs
Available on iTunes, CD Baby, anniejdahlgren.com
Fortunes Made
A Better Life
All Through the Night
Alley Cat

Feature Film
The Bet (co-writer)

Audio Plays
Fortunes Made

Musical Theater
Moment of Truth
(book)

Award-winning Screenplays
Sisters of Mercy
Too Tall Townsend

Deceivers (co-writer)
The Bet
Spirit Guides
Vigilance
New Texacornia

Music Video Productions
YouTube: Search on "Over 40 Productions"

Contact Annie at www.anniejdahlgren.com

Neal Graffy

"Delightfully unfettered by convention" pretty much sums up Neal Graffy's approach to history. Whether it be in print, radio, television, documentary or live, his audiences always find his presentations to be entertaining, fun and still educational.

Neal first gave voice to history in 1989 when he premiered a slide show talk on Santa Barbara History. Encouraged by the response, more talks were developed; and currently there are twenty different topics that have been presented in well over 250 shows.

Expanding from solo presentations, Graffy has had numerous appearances on local, state and national radio and TV including Huell Howser's *California's Gold*, KCET TV's *Life and Times* and nationally on *This Old House*. He has been featured in several documentaries including the Emmy Award winning *Impressions in Time*.

In addition to books on Santa Barbara history, he has authored numerous monographs for historical organizations, as well as articles in regional and national publications.

For fun, he collects Santa Barbara memorabilia and postcards, photographs, plays guitar, plus enjoys cruising around town in his unrestored 1941 Packard 180 limousine.

OTHER PROJECTS by Neal Graffy

Current Publications
Santa Barbara Then & Now
Street Names of Santa Barbara
Historic Santa Barbara

Forthcoming Publications
The Great Santa Barbara Earthquake -
  The Disaster that Built a City
Santa Barbara's Grand Hotel –
  The Potter
History Under Your Nose

A Partial List of Lectures
A Liar, A Drunk and a Piano Teacher -
  The Story of the Flying 'A' Studios
Santa Barbara's Grand Hotel -
  The Potter
Santa Barbara Then & Now

Montecito's Hilltop Barons
The Great Santa Barbara Earthquake -
  The Disaster That Built a City
Streets Names of Santa Barbara
Two Hotels and a Theater - The Story
  of the Arlington
History Under Your Nose
Fiestas, Festivals and Parades --
  Santa Barbara Celebrates!
Naples - A Tale of Two Cities
Santa Barbara's Powerful Women
Why Santa Barbara?
Fremont, Foxen & the San Marcos Pass
Norton I - The Forgotten Emperor
  of the United States
E Clampus Vitus – No Known Cure
Goleta – In Search of History
Santa Barbara – The Search for Water

Contact Neal at www.elbarbareno.com

Coming next...

An Unfortunate
Incident at Castle Rock

Coming so early in the morning, the sound of the clanging telephone startled Leontine and she spilled several drops of tea on her embroidered white linen table covering. Initially the novelty of having a telephone in one's own home was compelling and both she and Daisy would leap up with the first chime and offer bright greetings in lyrical tones to whomever was initiating the connection. Fairly rapidly however, Leontine had become less entranced. She grew increasingly resentful of the thing, elbowing its way into her day unbidden and demanding immediate attention. In nearly every instance the call was for Daisy in any case and when one happy day it occurred to Leontine that she could simply ignore it, that is mostly what she did.

She glanced at the wooden clock resting on the hall table. Not yet eight o'clock. The early hour implied some level of urgency. Leontine lifted the cylindrical receiver from its metal ring and raised the tulip of the mouthpiece to hover at neck level. "Good morning. This is Miss Birabent," she said to the device.

"Good morning, Miss Birabent, it's Nicholas Denman," said the tinny voice in her ear.

"Dr. Denman, I trust your day is going well."

"Actually, I was hoping I might trouble you to look after Patrick for a few hours. He has had quite a morning. There's s been an incident I'm afraid. An unfortunate incident at Castle Rock..."